A

Patron

Saint

for

Junior

Bridesmaids

Also by Shelley Tougas

The Graham Cracker Plot

Finders Keepers

A
Patron Saint
for
Junior Bridesmaids

Shelley Tougas

Roaring Brook Press
New York

Text copyright © 2016 by Shelley Tougas
Published by Roaring Brook Press
Roaring Brook Press is a division of Holtzbrinck Publishing Holdings Limited Partnership
175 Fifth Avenue, New York, New York 10010
mackids.com

Library of Congress Cataloging-in-Publication Data

Names: Tougas, Shelley, author.
Title: A patron saint for junior bridesmaids / Shelley Tougas.
Description: First edition. | New York : Roaring Brook Press, 2016. | Summary: Mary
   Margaret Miller is going to be a junior bridesmaid, but she is also having problems
   with school buly Brent Helzinski, and her cousin Eden, aka The Bride, is clashing
   with her mother about wedding plans.
Identifiers: LCCN 2016004841 (print) | LCCN 2016026467 (ebook) |
   ISBN 9781626724037 (hardback) | ISBN 9781626724044 (ebook)
Subjects: | CYAC: Bridesmaids—Fiction. | Weddings—Fiction. | Bullying—Fiction. |
   Family life—Fiction. | Christian life—Fiction. | BISAC: JUVENILE FICTION /
   Family / Marriage & Divorce. | JUVENILE FICTION / Religious / Christian /
   Values & Virtues.
Classification: LCC PZ7.T647155 Pat 2016 (print) | LCC PZ7.T647155 (ebook) |
   DDC [Fic]—dc23
LC record available at https://lccn.loc.gov/2016004841

Our books may be purchased in bulk for promotional, educational, or business use. Please
contact your local bookseller or the Macmillan Corporate and Premium Sales Department
at (800) 221-7945 ext. 5442 or by e-mail at MacmillanSpecialMarkets@macmillan.com.

First edition 2016
Book design by Andrew Arnold
Printed in the United States of America by LSC Communications US,
LLC (Lakeside Classic), Harrisonburg, Virginia

1   3   5   7   9   10   8   6   4   2

For Bob, Karen, and Cheryl, my patron saints
for great families

ABOUT BRENT HELZINSKI AND ME

I don't want to talk about Brent Helzinski.
Ever.

Part One

There's Going to Be a Wedding

Chapter One

There's going to be a wedding

To: bestgrandma@tricast.net, irishwill@tricast.net, maggiecollins@tricast.net, berniemiller@tricast.net, craigmiller@tricast.net, marymiller@tricast.net
From: edencollins@tricast.net
Subject line: News
Dear Grandma, Mom, Dad, Aunt Bernie, Uncle Craig, Mary, and Luke,
I am getting married. His name is Justin.

Sincerely,
Eden M. Collins

Someone hacked Eden's e-mail account. That's the only explanation. My cousin has never mentioned a guy—ever. She works in a hospital laundry to avoid people, and she takes college classes online for the same reason. Eden's social life revolves around church bingo with Grandma.

I start my computer's virus-scanning software in case I got infected by opening the message. Once Grandma replied to a scam e-mail about a Nigerian prince who needed money so he could hire a lawyer to collect his inheritance. She told the fake prince she'd be happy to help out as long as he paid her back. Aunt Maggie took her computer to a shop to have it cleaned up so the scammer couldn't get Grandma's personal information.

But my virus scan turns out okay. And all the e-mail addresses are correct. Everything looks normal. If this news is real, then Saint Anthony of Padua, the Patron Saint of miracles, had something to do with it. Church bingo is not a dating service.

Another e-mail pops into my account.

To: marymiller@tricast.net
From: edencollins@tricast.net
Subject line: Will you be my junior bridesmaid?

Dear Mary,

Grandma just replied to my e-mail announcing my wedding. She said I should ask you to be my junior bridesmaid because young cousins are perfect for that role. She asked about a maid of honor, and I don't plan on having one, so I guess you'll be both, in a way, if you know what I mean.

Will you be my junior bridesmaid?

Sincerely,

Eden M. Collins

So it is true! Eden's humor is straighter than uncooked spaghetti. If she doesn't joke about jokes, she definitely wouldn't joke about her own wedding. And she wants me to be a junior bridesmaid. I guess that means I'll get a pretty dress and matching shoes with heels. Maybe even a manicure! I've always wanted a real-deal manicure, the kind you see on models and rich ladies.

And then I think of something. Something that makes me smile really wide. I jump up from my desk, kneel down on the floor, and sweep my hand across the carpet under my bed until I find my notebook filled with Patron Saints. I flip through the pages until I find Saint Anthony of Padua, the Patron Saint of miracles. I put a big star next to his name because he's delivered two miracles. First, Eden is getting married, and second, the timing is perfect. Any minute now my principal will be calling Mom to tell her about my fight with Brent Helzinski. But surprise wedding news is way bigger than your never-in-trouble, straight-A daughter getting a week of detention.

I flip to a clean page in the notebook. After getting called to the school office today, I have a new saint to add to the notebook, a guy I'm going to need: Dominic Savio, the Patron Saint of juvenile delinquents. I make a star by his name and say a quick prayer. *Dear Holy Saint Dominic Savio, I guess I'm one of yours now. A juvenile delinquent! Me. The good kid. The principal said normally kids get suspended for fighting, but she's giving me a break because I never do stuff like that. Help! Brent is making me crazy!*

The phone rings. My whole body freezes. Downstairs Mom's voice is high pitched and happy, but I can't make out her words. Everything goes quiet, so I guess she hung up. High pitched and happy. That was not a call from my principal. My body relaxes, and I flop back onto my bed.

The phone rings again seconds later. This time her voice is deeper. During most of the call she's silent.

Seconds tick into minutes. Long seconds, long minutes.

Footsteps pound down the hall, and I sit up just in time to look casual before my bedroom door opens. Mom steps into the doorway, shaking her head and drilling her hands into her hips.

"I just had two very interesting phone calls."

"Oh?" I try to sound very innocent, but I'm not sure I'm succeeding. I'm an inexperienced juvenile delinquent.

"The first was Jon Hellmer," she says. Mr. Hellmer is the youth group director at our church. "Guess why he called?"

"Does he need me to volunteer for something? That's usually why he calls."

"No, that's not the reason. It seems he worked with Father Benson to nominate you for the Minnesota Church Youth Group Member of the Year Award. That award is based on integrity, volunteer service, and being a role model for younger kids. Integrity means being honorable and good." She crosses her arms. "You won the award. You know why that's ironic?"

Here we go.

"Why?" I ask.

"Less than sixty seconds later your principal called." Mom takes a deep breath. "She said you punched Brent Helzinski in the face. That is not integrity!" Her Pump Quick uniform shirt is untucked, and her hair hangs in a droopy ponytail. Since Dad moved to North Dakota for the new job, Mom always looks like she just rolled out of bed.

"I'm sorry. It's complicated, Mom."

She sighs, and the anger seems to float out of her body with her breath. "Why in the world would you punch Brent Helzinski? That boy has enough problems. His mom practically lives in the bar."

"He's a bully."

"Violence is never the answer. It's never an option, Mary."

"I'm sorry to interrupt, but I have something ginormously important to tell you." I take a breath and swoop in with my distraction. "Mom, Eden is getting married!"

"What?" She leans against the door, like she might fall over without support.

"You need to check your e-mail. She wrote to all of us. She's getting married to some guy named Justin."

Mom tightens her ponytail. Whenever she's nervous, she tugs at her hair. "Maggie would've told me."

"Aunt Maggie got the e-mail, too. We all did."

"Let me read it."

As she leans toward the computer screen, another e-mail from Eden lands in my inbox. Mom reads the new one out loud:

Dear Grandma, Dad, Mom, Aunt Bernie, Uncle Craig,
Mary, and Luke,
You are all probably wondering if Justin is Catholic.
The answer is no, but please don't worry. He is taking
classes to convert.

Sincerely,
Eden M. Collins

Mom looks as if she'd jump in the car and make the four-hour drive to Aunt Maggie's house if she could. She tucks in her work shirt. "I should call Maggie, but I don't want her to hear it from me. Leave it to Eden to send an e-mail. Who does that?"

"Eden. Eden does that," I say. "She wants me to be in the wedding."

"That'll cost a fortune."

"Do you want me to tell her no? She said that Grandma told her to ask me."

"Of course she did," Mom mutters. I can practically see images of expensive wedding dresses in her brain. Details of the Brent fight are evaporating, and my mood improves by 100 percent in seconds. Mom continues, "E-mail! That's no way to tell your family important news. We'll be to-gether next weekend for Easter. Why not tell us then?"

"Because it's Eden. She doesn't like talking when we're all together in a group. It makes her anxious."

"She didn't even tell us she had a boyfriend. This is crazy. Just crazy. Poor Maggie. And Uncle Will! It'll break his heart."

"Doesn't your shift start at four-thirty? You only have fifteen minutes."

Mom checks the time on her phone and shakes her head like she can't believe she's running late again. "Listen, Luke has a spelling test. Please go over his words. I didn't have a chance to get groceries because the guy was here fixing the furnace. Warm up the leftover meatloaf. Make sure you both eat a vegetable, too. And please fold the towels in the dryer."

"I will."

"And do your own homework."

"I know."

"And load the dishwasher if you've got time. Only if you have time. Homework first."

"I'll have time."

"Thanks, honey. I know I can count on you." She disappears into the hall, calling to Luke, "Mary's in charge. You need to listen to her." Then she pops back into my room. "If Dad calls, don't say anything about Eden. He didn't get the e-mail because he still doesn't have Internet at the motel."

"Why can't I tell him?"

"Once he hears about you being in the wedding, he'll just worry about how much it's going to cost."

"But what if he asks?"

Mom looks at me like I'm stupid. "He's not going to ask, 'Is Eden getting married?'"

"He'll say something like, 'What's new?'"

"Mary, I'm not saying it's a secret forever. Just tell him nothing is going on because, actually, nothing is really going on. It's not official news until I talk to Maggie, right? We don't even know if it's 100 percent true." If the Pope ever decides to pick a Patron Saint for Truth-Stretching, my mom will be a top candidate. She's the Master of the Not-Exactly-A-Lie.

"Okay."

With that final instruction, she leaves. The front door slams, and in seconds the car is rumbling. It rattles and coughs and stalls. The engine screeches as she starts it again, and the rumbling fades away.

I flop on the bed. Crisis averted! But at the back of my mind a question lingers: What mom forgets her daughter just punched a kid?

Even worse, what girl wins an award for being nice the same day she punches someone? What girl is proclaimed a junior bridesmaid hours after getting lectured in the principal's office?

Me—a responsible daughter, a sweet big sister, a devoted Catholic, the nicest girl in school. Mary Margaret Miller. The girl who knocked down the school's meanest bully with a mighty right hook.

ABOUT BRENT HELZINSKI AND ME

I DON'T WANT TO TALK ABOUT BRENT HELZINSKI.
I don't want to think about Brent Helzinski.
I don't want to text or post or e-mail about him.
Ever.

There's going to be a wedding . . . and gossip

BEFORE I GET TO MOM'S CHECKLIST, I COUNT THE number of stars I've made next to Saint Ann, Patron Saint of mothers, and compare it to the stars next to Saint Joseph, Patron Saint of fathers. The stars represent each time I've prayed to that particular saint. I've only been keeping the notebook since November, but Saint Joseph is definitely outpacing Saint Ann. I had to start an entire page just for Saint Joseph.

I don't love my dad more than my mom, but he's living alone in a crappy hotel room in North Dakota. I feel bad for him, and he's definitely less annoying than Mom with her constant to-do lists and complaints about being tired and sad, like she's the only one who misses Dad. When Dad got the new job, we took a family vote and decided Mom, Luke, and me would stay in Minnesota until the end of the school year and then join Dad. Plus new oil jobs are bringing so many people to North Dakota that he can't even find an apartment.

But that was our only vote.

We didn't get to vote on whether the massive Home Supply Station should be allowed to open in Holmestrand, even though my family's hardware store had been here for 100 years.

We didn't get to vote on where people in northern Minnesota shop for their tools, paint, extension cords, and nails.

We didn't get to vote on whether it was time to close our store or keep fighting Home Supply Station and its extra-low prices and huge inventory. We couldn't pay the bills, so there was no vote. The bank forced Miller Family Hardware to close.

Dad says we're lucky he got the oil job in North Dakota. It pays well, and we'll eventually get out of debt. North Dakota is cold and flat and empty. As far as you can see, there's nothing but dirt and sky. It's Minnesota without hills or trees or lakes. But some brainy engineer figured out how to pump oil from that empty land, and now we have to move to there.

I can't stand those engineers and the oil company and North Dakota. I flip through pages of Patron Saints and find where I'd written *Saint Mary, Queen of Peace, Patron Saint of North Dakota.* I scribble over the words, pressing so hard the tip of the pen rips through the paper. There weren't any prayer stars by her name, anyway.

Immediately, I feel bad for crossing out Saint Mary and taking her away from the North Dakotans. Nice girls don't take Patron Saints away from the people the Pope has assigned them to protect. I can't erase pen marks, so I write it on a fresh page, in my best handwriting:

Saint Mary, Queen of Peace,
Patron Saint of North Dakota.

And I say a quick prayer. *Dear Holy Saint Mary and Dear Holy Saint Ann, please help my mom be less stressed out in North Dakota. Make it a place where she's relaxed and happy like she used to be.*

There. One prayer gets a star for Mom and a star for North Dakota.

"What are you doing?" Luke peeks in my room. His chin is smeared with peanut butter.

"You're not supposed to eat peanut butter. We're supposed to eat meatloaf."

"What difference does it make?"

"Because Mom said so."

Luke jumps on my bed. His shoes are muddy, and he has peanut butter on his fingers, too. He's eight years old and always filthy, a magnet for dirt and crumbs and mysterious stains.

"Luke, you're making a mess."

"I heard Mom on the phone, and it sounds like you really walloped someone and I think it was that Brent guy with the greasy hair."

"It's none of your business," I say. "Get off my bed and do your homework. I mean it."

"Have you ever hit anyone before?"

"I'm going to hit you if you don't get off my bed."

I meant it as a joke, but it came out serious. Luke's smile disappears, and his eyes look surprised. This year I've tried extra hard to be nice to him because he really misses Dad. For Christmas he asked if his present could be legally changing his name to Craig Miller—our dad's name. That's some serious Dad-missing behavior.

Luke stomps out of my room, yelling, "You're a huge grump!"

"I'm sorry!" I call after him. "I'll give you an Oreo after we do your spelling words, okay?"

He sticks his head through the door. He's smiling again. "Can I have two? Or maybe three since you're so crabby?"

Mom will be mad if he has one, but I know Luke. He won't stop annoying me until he gets more. I pull the same distraction maneuver I used on Mom. "Guess what? Eden's getting married! And I'm going to be in the wedding!"

"Serious?"

"Totally. If you write her a note, like a congratulations kind of thing, I'll scan it into the computer and e-mail it to her. Then she can see your actual handwriting and how good it is."

He beams. "I'll do it right now."

As he scoots to his room, my phone buzzes. I have a text, and not just one. While I was talking to Mom, the messages were piling up. Looks like every kid in school is talking about Brent Helzinski and me.

Nadia Clonski: Just heard. What happened?

Abbie Greenfeld: Brent hit his face on your fist? ☺

Connor Lewis: WTH?

Shane Johnson: Mary "The Fist" Miller!

Riley Nelson: OMG Mary!

Then my phone rings—a ring from an actual call, not a text. It's Jessica, my friend whose parents love love love the Home Supply Station. I know evidence when I see it. They have plastic bags from Home Supply Station at their house and receipts on the kitchen counter.

I answer at the last second. "Hey, Jess."

"Oh my God, Mary! What happened today? I mean, I heard what happened. But why?"

"It's so not a big deal."

"You got in a fight. A real fight! That's a big deal."

"I'll tell you about it later." I say this even though I don't plan to tell her about it *ever*. "So you know my cousin Eden?"

"The one who's weird because of that disorder thing?"

"Social anxiety disorder. She's not weird. She just acts weird because of her disorder."

"Isn't that what I said?"

"Not exactly."

Jessica sighs into the phone. "Okay, okay. What's going on with your cousin Eden?"

"She's getting married, and I get to be in the wedding."

"Cool!" Jessica gushes. "What's your dress going to look like?"

Big *whew*. Mom, Luke, and now Jessica. This distraction thing really works.

ABOUT BRENT HELZINSKI AND ME

IT'S A SIN TO HAVE HATE IN YOUR HEART.

Therefore, the feeling I have for Brent Helzinski is strong dislike.

Chapter Three

There's going to be a wedding . . . and a confession

TWO DAYS. THAT'S HOW LONG IT TAKES MOM TO REMEM-ber I walloped Brent. I avoided the subject for two whole days, but instead of two days of relief it was two days of worrying. I've been constantly on edge wondering when she would bring it up. And all I did was think about what she'd say and how I'd explain it. That was the hardest part, because I can't explain what I don't understand.

When Mom finally confronts me, she doesn't even give me a lecture. Instead, she says, "After school, you're going to hop on your bike and go straight to church for Confession."

And that's worse than a lecture. It's worse than being

grounded. I'll have to look into the eyes of Father Benson, who nominated me for that youth group award. I've always been his favorite kid. I volunteer in the church day care and help with the food shelf drive. Three years in a row, I was Mary in the Children's Christmas Pageant. Jessica was so jealous. One year, she had to play one of the three wise men. Wearing a fake beard, Jessica brought baby Jesus the gift of myrrh. Myrrh! What even is that?

So I've gone from playing Mary the Mother of God to Mary the Puncher of Brent.

As I bike to church, I think about cruising around town for an hour, then going home and pretending I was at Confession. Mom would never know because Confession is supposed to be private—just you, the priest, and God. But Holmestrand is so small she'd probably find out. Secrets here are like lice. They spread from person to person until everyone is scratching. I'd be lying, which is a sin, and dishonoring my mother, which is also a sin. A sin wrapped in another sin.

Father Benson and I sit across from each other in a small room next to the altar. He has a round face, thick silver hair, and a wide smile that shows all his teeth, which are yellow and crooked. It'd be vain to whiten them, I guess, and being vain is a sin, but probably not as big a sin as punching someone.

My normal confession is always the same: I read books past bedtime. That's what I tell him because the real stuff is too awful for the nicest girl at St. Bridget, the girl who won the state award. I can't tell him I copied part of an essay off the Internet. It was just once, and *only* because I forgot it was due the next day, and I'll never do it again. I can't tell him about wanting to throw a rock at Jessica's family car when I saw a Home Supply Station bag in the back window. I can't tell him about Brent.

Here's the thing, though: If you go to Confession with a real sin, like cheating in school, and you don't actually confess it, you no longer have one sin. Now you have two! Cheating in school *and* the sin of omission, which is keeping your sin a secret. Not telling is just as sinful as sinning. So technically I sin every time I come to Confession! I can't think about it. All these sins are too heavy for my heart, and there are so many piled up that if I dwell on one thing too long, I might explode.

Besides, I've done something that's way, way worse than the sin of omission.

I quit praying to God.

I can never tell Father Benson—or anyone—that I don't

pray to God anymore. They would never think the same of me ever again. So I keep that confession in the darkest part of my heart.

When I'm in the room with Father Benson, I always say, "Bless me Father for I have sinned. I stayed up past bedtime reading a book." Father Benson laughs and asks, "Was it the Bible?" And I always give him the name of some random book. And he always says, "I absolve you from your sins. In the name of the Father, the Son, and the Holy Spirit. Amen."

This time, though, when I mumble, "Bless me Father for I have sinned," I can't spit out more words. I stare at the carpet, which is frayed and dirty but can't be replaced because people don't put enough money in the donation baskets, according to Father Benson. When people pass the baskets during mass, and there's the clink of coins instead of the swish of paper money, Father Benson's crooked teeth disappear under thin lips.

That's how he looks now. Thin lips.

"Please continue," he says.

"Let me think about it."

He lets me think for a minute. Then he sighs and says, "I already know, Mary. I heard from the school secretary's husband's cousin's wife at the café this morning."

See? Lice!

"Tell me what happened, Mary," he says. "God is forgiving. I can feel His love for you in this room."

I close my eyes and try to feel His love. How is His love supposed to feel? Like a soft breeze? A shiver? A wave of warmth? I just feel me with my sweaty hands and burning stomach.

"Excuse me, Mary," Father Benson asks. "Are you paying attention?"

"Yes."

"Tell me what Brent did to provoke you."

I keep my eyes down and stay quiet.

"Mary, bullies are a fact of life. But Jesus commands us to turn the other cheek. We also must love our neighbor. Of course, when the neighbor is a bully, it isn't easy. Turning the other cheek is never easy, especially when you live an honorable life."

I nod.

"You are probably wondering, 'How do I defend myself against bullies if I'm supposed to turn the other cheek?' That is an excellent question." He looks proud of himself as he delivers the answer. "You defend yourself by praying to God for Jesus to defend you."

"Okay."

"Do you have any questions, Mary?"

"No."

He watches me for a moment and presses his glasses up his nose. "Are you sure?"

I feel a spark in my guilty heart and suddenly I hear myself saying, "Jesus got angry sometimes." I'd been *thinking* those words; then they just flew out of my mouth. I focus on staring at my lap. I'm totally embarrassed.

He adjusts the white priest's collar on his shirt and says, "Yes, that's true. But His anger was honorable because He was deeply concerned about acts against God. Also, He controlled His anger. His anger didn't control Him."

I nod even though this makes no sense whatsoever.

"I'll give back that youth group award. I don't deserve it."

"No, that award is yours. And your story is a good one because it shows that good people sin, but we can all repent because God is forgiving."

"Oh."

Father Benson says, "Let's bow our heads and pray together."

He bows his head and prays.

I bow my head, too. I listen to Father Benson's words, but in my heart, I'm not praying. Technically speaking, I didn't confess. Father Benson guessed.

• • •

I stopped praying to God and started the Patron Saints notebook after Ryan Dorman's Halloween party, the night everything changed.

The timing went like this:

I went to Ryan's party Saturday night.

I came home and heard about the plane crash.

I started my notebook of Patron Saints.

The party was awful because Brent Helzinski came. Ryan's parents must have told him to invite the whole class, because who'd voluntarily put Brent on a party list? Kindergartners wouldn't invite Brent to a party even if he promised to bring ponies.

After the Halloween party, I went straight to my room and got ready for bed. I could hear my parents mumbling—their voices serious and quiet—and I figured it was another money conversation. When I walked into the kitchen to say good night, I heard Mom say, "You see this stuff on the news, but you never think you'll have a connection to it."

"To what?" I asked.

Dad said, "You were pretty young when John Danner worked at Dave's Diner. Do you remember him?"

"The guy with the goofy laugh. I remember. He moved to Florida."

"John and his wife were on that plane that crashed in the Caribbean."

"I didn't know there was a plane crash," I said. "When did it happen?"

"This morning. He was on vacation with his wife," Mom said. "We're going to take up a collection at church for his children. Pray for them, okay?"

"I will." I remembered that John Danner was tall and thick and fierce-looking, but he laughed like a toddler—high-pitched and silly. I pictured John and his wife laughing on the plane, and I imagined John's goofy laugh turning to a desperate, unanswered prayer.

The thought made me shiver.

Mom said, "It's late. We can talk more tomorrow. Time for bed."

"Can I go online and read the news story?"

"Sure, but only for a few minutes." Dad hugged me. "See? Our troubles are nothing. We should count our blessings every day."

My parents went to bed, and I got on my laptop. The news articles said investigators didn't know why the plane crashed. They would be sweeping the ocean floor to find the plane's black box, which stored information about the plane and the flight. John and his wife's names were among those in a list of passengers. Dad's words echoed in my head. *Our troubles are nothing.*

That's when I figured it out: God didn't answer our prayers to save the hardware store because our prayers were *nothing.* A joke. If He's not saving people from plane crashes, why would God care about a stupid hardware store in northern Minnesota? There are wars and climate change and kids with awful diseases. How could God hear the prayers of sick kids with all the noise from people whining about nothing?

My prayers are tiny. They've always been tiny. I used to pray for Santa to bring the presents I wanted. I wasted a whole prayer on a My Best Friend Doll! God gets ridiculous prayers from ridiculous people all day, every day. Prayers from hockey players wanting to win a game, prayers from a girl hoping a boy likes her, prayers from hunters hoping to shoot sixteen-point bucks.

I realized I'd been doing it wrong. I went back to my room, got a notebook, and spent an hour looking up Patron Saints on the Internet. I knew the famous Patron Saints, like Saint Jude for lost causes and Saint Francis for animals. But there are *hundreds* of Patron Saints, and each one is a specialist. They have time for tiny prayers because they aren't watching out for the whole world. Saint Mary, Queen of Peace, pretty much has nothing to do except take care of North Dakota. She doesn't have to worry about war and plane crashes. Just North Dakota.

Grandma has asked Patron Saints for help. She wanted to sell her house so she could move in with Aunt Maggie and Uncle Will. She got a statue of Saint Joseph, the Patron Saint of households, and buried it in her yard. Then the house sold, and she said it was because of Saint Joseph. She also told me that Saint Gertrude of Nivelles, Patron Saint of cats, helped her find Cleocatra when she escaped from the house.

Grandma says her small prayers to the Patron Saints. Sometimes it even works.

The first saint in my notebook is Saint Sebastian, Patron Saint of hardware stores. It was too late, but I needed to see his name on paper.

ABOUT BRENT HELZINSKI AND ME

I CAN THINK OF ONE PERSON WHO LOVES BRENT Helzinski. Jesus. Jesus loves Brent Helzinski because Jesus loves everyone.

Oh, and Brent Helzinski's mother. She probably loves Brent, too.

Chapter Four

There's going to be a wedding . . .
and a change in plans

I'M PACKING MY BAG FOR EASTER AT AUNT MAGGIE AND Uncle Will's house when Mom comes into my room and says, "We're not going. I'm too tired for a long drive."

We never miss Easter at Aunt Maggie's. Two years ago we drove through a spring blizzard. We risked our lives for ham and cheesy potatoes, and now we can't go because she's tired? I don't get it. Luke runs down the hall to my room and says, "Did you say we're not going?"

"Sweetie, I'm exhausted."

"How will the Easter Bunny know where to find me? We're always in St. Paul for Easter."

Mom says, "The Easter Bunny knows these things."

"What about the wedding?" I ask. "We're supposed to talk about it. We don't know when it's going to be, we don't know where it's going to be, and I don't even know what a junior bridesmaid does."

Luke stomps his foot. "The Easter Bunny has never been to this house!"

"Go write a letter and explain," Mom says. "The Easter Bunny will understand. I'll sign it, too."

Luke thinks this is a great idea. "Then I can tell him exactly what kind of candy I want!"

"Maybe the Easter Bunny has already picked out the candy," Mom says. "Maybe the Easter Bunny doesn't have time to shop."

Mom needs help, so I say, "You don't want to be rude and greedy, Luke."

Luke nods and races to his room to write his letter. I'm not sure how bunnies got tangled up with Easter and Jesus's resurrection. Jelly beans and a crucifixion? It's a question for Saint Dymphna, Patron Saint of insanity.

"You're the best big sister." Mom hugs me. "I'm sorry about changing our plans, but I just can't do it this year."

"What about the wedding plans? You said it was fine for me to be in the wedding. Are you changing your mind?"

"Not at all. I should've said yes immediately. Family is

more important than money." Mom squeezes my shoulder. "I'm sorry you're disappointed. But how about this—we'll order pizza tonight! Tomorrow I'll make tacos and cake, and on Easter we'll eat all the leftovers after church and watch movies."

"But I gave up pizza for Lent."

Her shoulders drop, and she sighs. "Mary, I'm not cooking tonight. I worked ten hours, and there's no food in the house. I'll get groceries in the morning."

"You could get groceries tonight."

"Are you not hearing me? Tonight it's pizza. Pick off the pepperoni. Then you can feel like you're still giving up something."

"Mom, it's Friday! You and Luke can't have meat on Friday during Lent."

She tugs at her ponytail and sighs. "We'll get plain cheese pizza. You can have peanut butter toast."

"Okay." It's going to be hard to eat peanut butter toast while Mom and Luke have pizza, but I'll get the leftovers. "Why do Catholics have so many rules?"

"All churches have rules."

"Why do we have so many saints? Jessica says Lutherans focus on Jesus and that all those saints take away attention from Jesus, which is a bad thing."

"Honey, I'm too tired to talk about religion. This sounds like a conversation for Grandma."

Luke comes back into my room and says, "Before we eat we have to talk to Grandma and tell her we're not coming."

"Later." Mom rolls her eyes. "I'm not in the mood."

"But I already called her on the computer so we can see her and talk to her and tell her that we can't come for Easter."

"She's on the computer right now?" I ask.

"She's waiting."

Mom looks like she wants to beat her head against the wall. If Mom wasn't so stressed out, I'd laugh. Luke does not understand our family at all. We follow Luke to the kitchen where Grandma's face fills the laptop screen. I can see the frown through her silver bangs. Mom tugs her ponytail and plops down on a chair like a kid who knows she's in trouble.

"What's this I hear about you not coming? I'm making a German Easter. Rouladen and potato dumplings and a black forest cake." From behind Grandma I see Uncle Will, Eden's dad and Aunt Maggie's husband. He shouts from across the kitchen, "And I'm making Irish soda bread so there's something decent to eat!"

Grandma shouts back, "I'm making dinner rolls that don't taste like paste!" This is part of Easter in our family; Grandma and Uncle Will constantly argue about whose heritage is superior—his Irish or her German.

"Maybe you can freeze leftovers for us," Mom says. "I'm sorry, but I'm sick."

Mom's story is shifting from being "tired" to being "sick," because being tired is never an excuse for Grandma. She'd tell Mom to load up on coffee and get in the car.

"Do you have a fever?" Grandma leans closer and inspects Mom's face.

Luke puts his hand on Mom's forehead. "She feels fine to me."

"I think I'm coming down with something that will hit later." Mom waves Luke's hand away. "These bugs always start with being tired."

"Mary, does her forehead feel warm to you?"

I put my hand against Mom's forehead. Of course it's completely normal, but I don't know what to say. Lying is a sin, but if I tell the truth, Grandma will get mad at Mom, and then Mom will get mad at me. She'll either have to drive to St. Paul or turn her truth-stretching to an outright lie. As far as I know, she flat-out lied only once, and it backfired. Mom didn't want to go to a family baby shower, so she told Grandma she had to work. Grandma found out and didn't speak to Mom for two months. She sent Mom a birthday card and wrote, "I hope you have a happy birthday and that is not a lie because I don't lie to family. XOXO. Love you!"

Finally I say, "I don't know. My hand is too cold."

When Grandma swipes at her bangs, she leaves a trail of flour across her forehead. "When are we going to see you? You said you'll be working weekends at the station all spring, and if you move to North Dakota right after school ends, it'll be months before we have a real visit."

"Months?" Luke shouts. "No way!"

"We'll work something out," Mom says.

I offer a compromise. "Maybe we can spend some time in St. Paul on our way to North Dakota."

"Great idea!" Mom says.

"I certainly hope so." Grandma sighs. "I'm crushed—absolutely crushed—that we can't be together. Since you didn't have a First Communion party for Luke, which also crushed me, by the way, I was looking forward to taking him to Easter mass and witnessing him get Communion on the Holiest Day of the Year."

Grandma's words make Mom freeze. Luke's First

Communion—that's her worst rubber-band stretch ever. Mom pulled him out of First Communion classes because she was too busy to take him. She said he could do it next year when we're with Dad again. She let Grandma believe he got First Communion, because Grandma is old-fashioned about church stuff. Catholic kids are supposed to get their First Communion when they can tell the difference between the Communion wafer and regular old bread. Mom says she'll tell Grandma about the delay eventually, but since there's no reason to mention it *right now*, we shouldn't mention it *right now*.

And suddenly I realize something. We're not skipping Easter in Minneapolis because Mom's tired. She wants to cancel Easter because we'd all go to church, and Luke wouldn't take Communion, and Grandma would know the truth. Stretch goes the rubber band!

We've been quiet a long time. Luke wiggles around, and I can tell he's about to say something, so Mom clears her throat and says, "You're starting to freeze up, Mom. I think we're losing the connection."

Then she snaps the laptop shut and says, "Blasted Internet connection!"

"Our Internet has the worst timing," I say, and Mom gives me a knock-it-off look. As she leans back in the chair, I notice the circles under her eyes. She really and truly is tired. I immediately feel bad about the whole deal—for Mom's dark circles and for truth-stretching with Grandma. I rush to my room to put stars on both of their pages.

ABOUT BRENT HELZINSKI AND ME

BRENT HELZINSKI LEFT A ROTTEN APPLE ON MY DESK with a note that said, *apples are red and your eyes are blue and this apple is rotten and so are you.*

My eyes are brown.

He's so dumb.

Chapter Five

There's going to be a wedding . . . and a detour

Six weeks after Easter, right before we're supposed to finish school and leave Holmestrand, Mom announces Luke and I are taking a detour. A big detour. We're going to spend the summer in St. Paul.

"We still don't have a place to live, and I need to find a job," Mom says. "We can't have you alone all day in a new town. So you're going to stay with Aunt Maggie and Uncle Will." She smiles and claps her hands together like this is the best news.

I should've guessed something was up. Normally Mom sits on the couch and talks to Dad on the phone. But lately she's been taking the phone into their bedroom and closing the door. The detour messes up everything. I need to make at least one friend this summer, otherwise I'll be sitting alone at lunch on the first day. The thought makes my stomach burn.

Luke looks shocked. "But I want to see Dad!"

"I know. And Dad wants to see you. But it's the hand we've been dealt, so we have to make it work." Mom pulls him into a snuggle. "You get to hang out with Grandma. She's got so many plans already. Waterparks and the zoo and the Children's Museum."

"Grandma's already made plans?" Luke stomps his foot. "When were you going to tell us?"

"I'm telling you now."

I say, "But I need to meet people before school starts."

"Mary, this means you get to be actively involved with the wedding." Mom's voice is all sunshine. "Dress shopping and looking at flowers and all that fun stuff."

"Maybe they won't do that this summer. It took Eden twenty years to meet a boyfriend. Maybe it'll take her another twenty to set a wedding date."

"Please don't argue with me," Mom says. "I'm not happy about it, either, but we have to do our best to get through it. All of us."

"If you're not happy about it, and Luke's not happy

about it, and I'm not happy about it, then why are we doing it?"

"Your dad thinks this is the best option." Now Mom's trying to run from it and blame Dad.

I cross my arms. "Don't we get a vote?"

"I want a vote!" Luke stomps his foot again.

"Mary, I need you to set an example for Luke. It's already hard. Don't make it harder."

I want to run to my room and slam the door, but I can't. Luke would copy me, and the dark circles under Mom's eyes would get darker, and it'd be my fault. Mom squeezes my hand. "Will you try to make this work? Please?"

I wonder if there's a Patron Saint for Kids Who Get No Say in Their Own Lives. I grit my teeth and force my head to nod.

Mom's face relaxes, but Luke isn't ready to give up. "We want a vote. Right, Mary?"

I can barely form words, but I manage to say, "Waterparks and the zoo. It'll be fun."

"So much fun. And all the planning with the wedding! It'll be a wonderful summer." Mom smiles and looks at me, which is my cue to show Luke I agree. I force another nod. It's the best I can do.

· · ·

Jessica comes to see me the morning we're leaving. She hands me a gift wrapped in silver foil with a red ribbon. "Here. For you."

"I have something for you, too."

We go to my bedroom and swap gifts. She gives me a teddy bear with "Friends Forever" stitched on its tummy. I give her a framed picture of us from her last birthday party. We're wearing plastic tiaras and making weird faces.

Jessica says, "We'll talk online at least once a week, right?"

"Sure." My eyes sting. "More than once a week. I want to hear everything about soccer and when you're going to the lake and Nadia Clonski's birthday party."

"Maybe you can come back for her party. You should ask your mom."

It sounds like the kind of thing Mom would promise I can do but not deliver. "Okay. I'll try."

Luke runs through the door and jumps next to Jessica. "Did you bring me a present?"

"Sorry, Luke." She gives his shoulder a little punch. "I have an old cough drop in my pocket. Want that?"

"You can still buy something for me and mail it."

"Luke!" I say. "Go."

"But I want to say goodbye," he whines.

"Go. Or I'll write a letter to the Pope."

Luke races out of my room without another word. Jessica laughs. "He's still afraid of the Pope?"

"The Pope works better than threats about Santa Claus, which is weird, because they're both old men in funny costumes."

Jessica takes a tissue from the box on my desk, wipes her eyes, and then hands one to me, too. "So what's up with this wedding? Do you have pictures of dresses?"

"Not yet."

"I was a flower girl when I was five. That was easy. I just had to look cute. A bridesmaid has to throw a bachelorette party, but you're not old enough to go to a bar and dance."

"Eden won't want a party. She definitely wouldn't go to a bar and dance."

"Brides like attention. Even shy brides act like princesses."

"Not Eden," I say. "She won't have a bachelorette party. I'll be surprised if there're more than twenty people at the wedding."

Mom yells from the living room. "Mary! Jessica's mother is here."

We go to the living room where Mom pulls Jessica into a hug. Jessica's mom hugs me, too, but I pull away quickly. I haven't forgotten the Home Supply Station bags in her car and the receipts on her kitchen counter. Then Luke hugs everyone, including Mom and me.

Luke sniffles and says, "You should visit us in North Dakota. It's just like Minnesota except without hills and trees and lakes." I glare at Luke. That's my line. Obviously he's been eavesdropping again.

Our moms laugh, and I mess up his hair. "Watch out," I say. "You'll grow up and become the governor of North Dakota."

"Probably," he says.

Jessica and her mom wave from the car as they drive away.

I can't wave back. My arms are too heavy. I whisper to Luke, "Blow them kisses."

He kisses both of his palms and blows toward the car. He does it over and over, until the car turns left at the stop sign and disappears.

ABOUT BRENT HELZINSKI AND ME

BRENT HELZINSKI CAME WITH HIS STEPFATHER TO OUR going-out-of-business sale. I was taking apart empty shelves on the back wall. Brent bumped into me and said, "Hairy Mary's hardware store. Half the quality; twice the price."

Chapter Six

There's going to be a wedding . . . and a cute neighbor

EDEN'S BEDROOM GOT A MAKEOVER. LAST I SAW IT—AND it's probably been two years since I've actually gone into her bedroom—she was living in a sea of pinks and purples. Now the walls are light gray. She hung blue curtains and put white-and-blue comforters on each twin bed. She replaced movie posters with nature prints. It's a room for a grown-up, for a twenty-one-year-old bride-to-be.

When Eden was in middle school, I was in kindergarten, so it's not like we ever gabbed about teenage stuff like boys and music. We did puzzles and baked cookies. Grandma bought paint sets, and the three of us set up a little art studio in the basement. Then in high school Eden started working in the hospital laundry on weekends. After she graduated, she worked full time plus added online college classes. For the last five years, she's rarely been home during our weekend visits, and she never has time to come to Holmestrand.

Now we're roommates, and I don't know what to expect. Does she listen to hip-hop all night? Does she knit scarves or read magazines or play solitaire? Is she mad I'm crashing her space? Better me than Luke, who leaves a trail of cracker crumbs everywhere he goes. He'll be camping out at Grandma's. When Grandma retired, Aunt Maggie and Uncle Will changed their two-story house to a duplex so Grandma could move in with them but have her own space. A door in the kitchen connects the two sides. Aunt Maggie and Uncle Will's side only has two bedrooms, which is why I'm bunking with Eden. Luke is staying in Grandma's extra room.

I unpack my clothes and set up my laptop. I put pictures of my soccer team and church youth group on the nightstand next to my rosary box. Grandma gave me the small box when I got my First Communion. It's made of dark, polished wood, and inside is a beautiful rosary necklace with a silver cross and blue beads. I hardly ever say rosary prayers because it takes forever, but I like the box. Also tucked inside is a pin with the face of Mary the Mother of God and a small prayer card with a picture of Pope Francis on one side and the Lord's Prayer printed on the other side.

I hear a whirring noise followed by a sputter. I look through the curtains and see a dark-haired boy in the yard pulling the cord on a lawn mower. After a few more coughs and sputters, he lets the cord snap and rubs his shoulder. He kneels by the mower and puts his head close, like it might whisper to him.

Customers used to bring lawn mowers to the store when they couldn't get them running. I knew how to change spark plugs before I could do long division. I go down the stairs and rush through the living room, where Uncle Will is napping on the couch.

As I cross the yard, I say, "It's the spark plug."

The boy stands and squints through the sunlight. "Huh?"

"It's probably a dirty spark plug."

He grins. "Are you the world's youngest mechanic?"

"My family owns a hardware store. Owned, I mean. I've seen a million lawn mower problems."

"Hardware stores fix lawn mowers?"

"In a small town, hardware stores do everything. You need help?"

He pretend kicks the mower. "Isn't it obvious?"

"Hang tight." I get a socket wrench from the garage. I kneel next to the lawn mower and twist the wrench until the spark plug comes out. I show him the plug. "See? Full of gunk. You need to scrape that off and clean it."

"Clean it with what? Regular soap?"

"Carburetor cleaner would work."

Now he looks at me suspiciously. "You're not going to steal my gig, are you? I made a lot of money mowing the lawn for Will Collins last year. The only other job in this neighborhood is babysitting for the kid on the corner. Braden. He's a monster. I'd rather sweat gallons mowing lawns than watch that kid."

I could use some cash, but my parents wouldn't let me take money for helping Aunt Maggie and Uncle Will.

"I don't want your mowing job. Promise."

Truth is, the yard needs more than a quick cut. Dandelions are scattered on the lawn like yellow confetti. Weeds sprout from the cracks in the sidewalk, and quack grass is weaving itself from the curb to the porch. Uncle Will is an over-the-road trucker. He drives across the country all week. When he's home, he's too tired for yard work, which is a man's job, according to Grandma.

The boy asks, "Do you live around here?"

"This is my aunt and uncle's house. I'm here for the summer, but trust me, the mowing job is yours."

"Good. But you can take Braden The Child Terrorist if you want. What's your name?"

"Mary Miller."

"I'm Nicholas Dang."

"Did you say Dang, like *dang it?*"

"It's common in Vietnam. Like Johnson or Smith," he says. "My parents call me Nicholas, but everyone else calls me Nick."

I'm glad he mentioned Vietnam because I was too embarrassed to ask. I would've guessed Chinese. Kids in St. Paul probably can tell the difference in Asian backgrounds, but pretty much everyone in Holmestand is as white as bleached T-shirts.

He asks, "Can you help me find some carburetor cleaner?"

"I'll be right back." I search the shelves in the garage until I find carburetor cleaner tucked behind bags of birdseed. Then I show Nick how to clean the spark plug. Thankfully I can just demonstrate and not talk because I'm running out of things to say. I'm shy, but not Eden-level shy. She takes medication for her disorder, which makes it hard for her to be in groups or around strangers.

I've seen it. She sweats and blushes and whispers, and words tumble out of her mouth in the wrong order. I overheard Aunt Maggie tell Mom that she even gets diarrhea. Eden isn't like that one-on-one with family, but all of us together are too much. At Sunday dinner or holidays, she tries to blend into the wall. How'd she ever go on a date?

Finally the spark plug goes back in its spot, and I hope it starts. I'll feel like an idiot if I'm wrong. "Let's try it."

"I got it," he says. "I can't let you do everything."

He yanks the cord. Nothing. The second time he yanks it coughs and sputters. The third time it roars. He smiles, yells *thanks* over the rumble of the motor, and starts cutting a strip of grass.

I go back to the house. They're going to call me in soon anyway. Grandma's planning a family meal for Justin tonight. Mom isn't leaving until morning, so we all get to meet him. I stop on the porch and watch Nick push the mower from the driveway toward the mailbox. The mower spits grass and weeds, leaving a lush strip behind him. It won't take long for the weeds to make a comeback, but for a day, the lawn will look perfect.

ABOUT BRENT HELZINSKI AND ME

I wasn't aiming at Brent. I kicked the ball hard because I wanted to score a run.

The ball blasted into Brent's face like it'd been shot from a cannon. Blood sprayed out of his nose and dripped down his chin. He dropped to his knees.

I said, "I'm sorry. I'm so sorry!"

He didn't answer, but his eyes said it all. I swear I saw a glint of fire.

A few weeks later, we both ended up at the Halloween party.

And everything changed.

Chapter Seven

There's going to be a wedding . . . really, really soon

FOR JUSTIN'S DINNER, WE'RE HAVING BEEF AND CABBAGE, German potato noodles, and streusel—all homemade by Grandma, of course. Normally we'd have a dinner like this on Sunday after church, not on a Friday, but Mom wants to leave in the morning for North Dakota.

"Mary," Grandma says, "use the good silverware."

Grandma is a kitchen tornado, checking the beef while putting frozen peas in a pan while searching for the fancy serving tray while issuing orders. Even though she's zipping around the hot kitchen, she looks perfect, like a model in a brochure for a retirement community. Her face is powder fresh, her floral dress is free of wrinkles, and her hair is tousled into soft curls. I think her energy comes from her Zumba class, but Dad says she runs off a nuclear core. He says, "Uncontained nuclear energy is toxic, you know." Then Mom smacks his shoulder and he laughs.

I set the table and sneak outside before I get another assignment. Eden is sitting on the wicker sofa on the screened-in porch. She looks like she's in a trance, petting Cleocatra and chewing the nail on her thumb. She doesn't notice me until I say hello.

When Eden stands and extends her arm, I think she's going to hug me, because everyone in our family hugs. By the time I realize she's only pointing at a dog on the sidewalk, I've got my arm on her shoulder. I pull away quickly, but she seems to realize this is a *hug*, so she comes toward me. We end up positioned with my nose in her ear.

I laugh, but Eden blushes. Her skin is clear and pale, so when she blushes, her face turns stoplight red. Maybe that's why she keeps her blond bangs too long and wears glasses with thick brown frames instead of contacts. She's hiding.

"Gosh, I haven't seen you since Christmas," Eden says. We always spend Christmas in St. Paul. Uncle Will won't visit us in the winter. He says he's afraid of polar bears, which cracks me up. Holmestrand is colder than St. Paul, but not by much.

"Can I see your ring?"

Eden blushes again. She sits on the wicker couch and puts her hand on her knee. The ring is gold with a diamond slightly bigger than a grain of salt. It's the perfect ring for her. She'd never wear flashy jewelry.

"It's pretty," I say.

She leans toward me and whispers, "Does it smell disgusting?"

"The ring? Rings don't smell."

"Not the ring. The food. Grandma asked what I wanted for dinner, and I know she loves making her German food, and I love eating her German food, so I said German food. But I didn't think about the smell of beef and cabbage."

I sit next to her. "Yeah, cabbage smells like someone forgot to take out the garbage."

"Do you think that's a bad first impression?"

"For Justin? I think he's going to have to get used to it."

She sighs. "You're right. I don't know why I'm so anxious. Why am I so anxious?"

"Probably because Uncle Will and Grandma are going to embarrass you. It's destiny. But he'll get used to it."

Eden nods and chews on her thumbnail.

"How did you meet him?"

"We met in my support group for social anxiety. I know it sounds weird that a bunch of people who can't function in social situations, and can't talk to other people, get together in a group to, well, talk about being unable to talk to other people. But it helps."

That's funny, but Eden speaks with such a flat voice that she's not funny even when she *is* funny.

"Did he ask you out? Or did you ask him?"

She blushes and shrugs.

"Oh, come on. You're going to be asked a million times. You might as well practice on me."

"Okay." She takes a deep breath, holds it for a moment, then exhales. "For a month we just smiled at each other. Then he said hello, so I said hello. Then after a few weeks, he asked how I was doing, and I said I was fine. A few weeks after that, he told me he had a good book about social anxiety, but he couldn't remember the title, so he asked for my e-mail so he could send me the information when he found the book. So we e-mailed for weeks. Long e-mails. Sometimes two or three a day."

"So did he ask you out? Or did you ask him?"

Another breath in, another breath out. "Grandma convinced me to ask him. She said he didn't ask for my e-mail because of a book. He wanted an excuse for us to write each other, and later he told me she was right." Eden smiles. "Grandma came on our first date because she wanted to make sure he wasn't a serial killer."

"Wasn't that weird?"

"Yes. And no. I was glad. She kept the conversation going."

"I'm surprised she didn't hire a private detective to investigate him."

"Hah! Guess what? She paid one of those online services to do a background check. Other than a parking ticket, it came back clean. But she made him promise to keep change in his glove compartment so he'll always have money for parking meters."

I know Grandma and Eden are tight, but boyfriend advice from grandmother to granddaughter seems weird even for them. Eden never had close friends, so Grandma would take her places Friday nights. I used to think Eden hated going to church bingo and classic movies and all-you-can-eat buffets. But now I get it. Eden didn't have anything else to do.

A car stops at the curb. I see a guy with dark hair and sunglasses at the wheel. He just sits there with the engine running. Eden sends Cleocatra into the house and says,

"That's Justin. I'm going to talk to him before he changes his mind and leaves. You should go inside. This might take a while."

Uncle Will thinks Eden is too young to get married, but Grandma thinks it's the greatest thing ever. Grandma and Uncle Will never agree. We're all Catholic, but they can't even agree about picking a church, which doesn't give me much hope for world peace. Uncle Will is Irish—100 percent—and he insists on going to St. Patrick, the Irish Catholic Church in St. Paul. Grandma is German, and she insists on going to St. George, the German Catholic Church, also in St. Paul. Since Grandma always wins, Aunt Maggie and Eden go to church with her at St. George, and Uncle Will goes alone to St. Patrick.

At holidays, Uncle Will makes Irish soda bread and Grandma makes *Wechen*, which are German dinner rolls. It's a bread standoff. Over flour and water! Uncle Will drinks Guinness beer—no need to mention it's Irish, right?—and Grandma will only drink Beck's. And when Uncle Will drinks too much Guinness, he slurs and pounds the table and reminds Grandma that Germany started all the wars and then lost them, and then she drinks more Beck's and says if the Irish could grow something other than potatoes, they wouldn't have starved 200 years ago. Every Christmas Dad says he wants to wrap up a package of screws and give them to Grandma and Uncle Will because they both have so many loose. I double-dog dare him to do it, but he just laughs.

Mom comes from the kitchen with glasses of water, which she sets by each plate. "Mary, look in the bureau for the nice cloth napkins. We're almost ready. I hope he gets here soon."

"He's in his car. Eden is talking to him. Did you know he has social anxiety, too?"

"Maggie told me," Mom says. "Honey, go outside and tell them dinner is ready."

Then the door opens, and Eden and Justin step inside. He has brown-framed glasses like Eden, but Justin is short and chubby. He's at least two inches shorter than Eden.

His lips form a stiff smile. "Hello."

Mom shakes his hand. "So nice to meet you."

In seconds we've all circled around him, except Grandma, who's getting food on the table. Justin turns licorice red when Aunt Maggie hugs him. He holds out his hand to Uncle Will and says, "Nice to meet you, sir." But Uncle Will shoves his hands in his pockets, grunts a hello, and looks away. Eden is sweating buckets. Mom already shook his hand, and Aunt Maggie hugged him, and Uncle Will is staring at the picture of Jesus next to the door. Nobody knows what to do. Justin's arm seems frozen, so I step between Uncle Will and Justin and grab Justin's hand like he'd intended to shake hands with me.

"Nice to meet you," I say in a very grown-up voice. This is my first real handshake outside of church and, I guess, my first real job as junior bridesmaid. I rescued Eden and Justin from an embarrassing Uncle Will moment.

Grandma calls us to the table.

"Before we eat, I have a surprise." Grandma claps her hands together. She takes a laptop from the bureau and turns it so we can see the screen.

It's Dad. He waves and says, "Hello everyone!"

I can tell Grandma's impressed with her technology skills. Her toothy grin stretches across her face. "We can't meet Justin without Craig!"

"Hi, Justin!" Dad waves. "Welcome to the family!"

"You, too!" Justin says and immediately turns red. "I mean, thanks and hello to you, too."

"What?" Dad says.

Luke sticks his face against the screen. "He said, 'You, too. I mean thanks, and hello to you, too.'"

Grandma puts the laptop on the corner of the table where there's an empty chair and says, "He's at McDonald's because they have wireless."

Dad waves French fries at us. When we start to pray, Dad bows his head right there at his table in McDonald's. In one quick mumble, we say, "BlessUsLordAndThese GiftsAmen." Justin's barely opened his mouth, and we're already past "amen" and eating. Grandma, Aunt Maggie, and Mom do their best small talk as dishes are passed around the table. They talk about Grandma's book club and North Dakota and Aunt Maggie's factory job and all the overtime she's working this summer.

Justin pushes food around his plate, taking only a few bites. Luke tells him, "Grandma's gonna get mad. You can't just eat the beef and not the cabbage even if the cabbage is disgusting."

The licorice color returns to Justin's face. Grandma shrugs like it's no big deal, even though we all know it's a very big deal to not like Grandma's food. Uncle Will says, "He doesn't like German food? Well, now! There's one thing I like about him."

"Will!" Aunt Maggie gasps.

"What? There's nothing wrong with liking one thing

about the guy. I just met him. It's better than finding a mountain of reasons to hate the boy."

"Dad," Eden says. "Don't be assuming German food is something not liked by Justin." Poor Eden. When her anxiety kicks in, her sentences come out in reverse, like Yoda.

Grandma scowls at Uncle Will. "Justin, don't pay any attention to him. Mister Shamrock here thinks the potato should be its own food group. You eat what you like."

Sweat is literally dripping down Eden's forehead. I don't think she can utter another sentence. I say, "Justin, Uncle Will makes the most amazing Irish food. Wait until you try his soda bread." That gets a little smile from Uncle Will, but Grandma frowns, so I add, "Personally beef and cabbage is my favorite meal." Then Uncle Will frowns. "But soda bread is my favorite bread." Grandma's frown deepens. "Streusel is my favorite dessert."

Dad's voice cuts through the silence. "I can't hear what you're saying. What'd you say?"

Uncle Will sort of shouts toward the laptop. "Justin likes Irish food."

"What?" Dad repeats.

Now Luke shouts, "Justin likes Irish food, but he hates

Grandma's beef and cabbage and Grandma's not even mad!"

"That's not what he said," I shout.

Mom leans toward the computer. "Mary was saying she loves Irish soda bread and streusel and pretty much everything that comes out of this kitchen. And Justin agrees. We all agree."

Justin stuffs a forkful of cabbage in his mouth and swallows without chewing. He looks at Uncle Will and says, "I like this meal, and I like potatoes, too. Very much."

Uncle Will points his fork at Justin and says, "Tell me something about yourself."

Justin's voice is quiet but steady. "I just graduated from the university."

"With honors! Isn't that wonderful?" Grandma asks nobody in particular.

"And?" Uncle Will's fork is still pointed at Justin.

"I'm going to graduate school for biomedical research."

"Isn't that fantastic!" Grandma says.

"And I've been accepted to the University of Illinois at Urbana-Champaign."

"Isn't it wonderful!" It's Grandma. Again.

"You're moving to Illinois?" Uncle Will smiles wickedly. "I'm sure my only daughter will miss you very much when you move."

"Obviously Eden is moving," Grandma says. "And we're thrilled she'll have this adventure and then move back to St. Paul because there are plenty of research jobs right here."

Uncle Will frowns while Aunt Maggie turns to Eden. "When were you going to tell us this?"

Eden's body seems to deflate. "Now is when I'm telling you." She looks like she just fell down a flight of stairs—embarrassed and injured and confused.

"Maggie, it sounds like she's going to move back." Mom pats Aunt Maggie's shoulder.

"Are you?" Aunt Maggie asks.

Eden nods and shrugs and shakes her head, so I'm not sure what the answer is. I look at Dad's face on the laptop. Usually he can turn our awkward family around when things get out of control, but he's sitting there with his eyes half closed, caught in a blink. Great. The connection froze.

Now what?

Aunt Maggie is just about to say something when Luke

starts coughing. Mom pats his back, and he spits a piece of beef on his plate. "You okay?"

Luke says, "Sorry but it's basically unchewable."

Everyone laughs, even Grandma and Uncle Will. Thank God for Luke. I promise a thank-you prayer to the Patron Saint of brothers or the Patron Saint of subject-changers, whichever is easiest to find.

"Luke, that's enough!" Mom tries to sound firm, but she's still laughing.

Grandma clears her throat. "Eden has some other news to share. First, she plans to stop going to college online. She's going to enroll in the university and finish her degree in Illinois. She'll attend classes with other students. Isn't that wonderful?" Eden looks relieved that Grandma's in charge.

Grandma continues, "Eden and Justin will be swamped with school, and of course they wouldn't dream of living together in a state of sin, so they will get married before school starts. That means we'll have a wedding on August nineteenth."

Aunt Maggie's mouth drops. "How is that possible?" She's not shocked that she's hearing these developments from Grandma—Grandma has always been Eden's spokesperson—she's shocked by the timeline. The date is ten weeks away. I don't know much about weddings, but my family spends more time planning Christmas. Grandma wants our wish lists by Halloween.

"I'll help," I say. Mom gives me a smile of approval.

"Eden says she doesn't want a splashy wedding," Grandma says, "but I'm going to do my best to make it spectacular."

"Spectacular isn't necessary," Eden says. "We—" Uncle Will cuts off Eden with a frown and a booming voice. "Parents need to plan for these things. We don't have thousands of dollars laying around. You'll be lucky to get spectacular hotdogs."

I need to turn Uncle Will's attitude around. He's embarrassing Eden. "Hotdogs could be fun, Uncle Will."

"Will you boil the hotdogs or grill them?" Luke asks. "I don't like black lines on hotdogs."

"Hotdogs will not be served at my granddaughter's wedding. I've lived in this house rent free for years, and God willing, for many more years to come. The least I can do is pay for this wedding. It'd give me untold joy to give Eden a spectacular wedding."

Spectacular. The word makes Eden cringe. Justin

squeezes her knee. Eden clears her throat and says, "We just want you and Justin's family. No fancy dresses or things that are fancy."

Justin nods. He nods and nods and nods.

"Don't be silly," Grandma says in her this-is-final voice. "You're going to have a real wedding. You deserve it."

Uncle Will chews while Aunt Maggie stares at her plate. Mom says, "A small wedding seems suited to Eden's personality."

Justin and Eden are both nodding now, so I say, "Yes, small. But spectacular, too. It can be both, right?"

Grandma acts like she didn't hear me. "Eden deserves a beautiful wedding with all of our friends and family, and that's exactly what she's getting. That's what grandmothers are for."

Luke says, "I wouldn't want a fancy dress, either."

"Of course not! You're a boy." Grandma rubs his shoulder. "But Eden is going to have a dress made for a princess. We'll go shopping as soon as possible. We're going to a dress shop—the kind that requires an appointment." Grandma's smile can't get any bigger. "We all have jobs to do. Luke, your job is to cooperate. Can you do that?" Luke nods, and Grandma turns stern eyes toward Uncle Will. "Shamrock, your job is to stay out of the way. Bernie, you'll be gone, and Maggie's stuck with overtime this summer. That means I'm counting on you, Mary."

"That's okay. I'll help. I'll even get a manicure if you want."

Grandma puts down her fork and clears her throat. "Being a junior bridesmaid is a solemn duty. It's more than pretty nails and a hairdo. By the way, nail polish is fine, but you're too young for lipstick, isn't she, Bernie?" Mom nods. "I'll have many jobs for you this summer."

I gulp. "Okay."

Grandma's not done. "Mary Margaret Miller, you will be Eden's right hand. You will be her support system. It's a big responsibility. We're all counting on you."

Immediately I think of my Patron Saints notebook and the wedding-related saints I'll need to add. A page for the bride, a page for the groom, a page for the caterer. I'm sure a page won't be enough for the Patron Saint of junior bridesmaids. She'll get her own notebook.

Part Two

There's Going to Be a Junior Bridesmaid

Chapter Eight

There's going to be a wedding in 64 days

THERE'S NO PATRON SAINT FOR JUNIOR BRIDESMAIDS.

How is that possible?

I've been on every Catholic website. There are Patron Saints for unmarried people, for engaged couples, for brides, for young brides, for grooms, for newlyweds, for good marriages, for difficult marriages.

Seriously? Marriage is one of the holiest sacraments in the Catholic Church. Marriage is so sacred the Church doesn't allow divorce! How can the Pope make a Patron Saint for everything related to weddings but miss junior bridesmaids?

I search Google for maid of honor and bridesmaid duties. Here's what I find: *The maid of honor is the bride's advocate. She provides emotional support during the many stressful moments and conflicts involved in wedding planning.* Stress and conflict—two things that freak me out. There's a huge list of duties, too. If there was a grown-up bridesmaid in the wedding, it'd be no big deal. I could be in charge of wearing a dress and holding flowers, and she could handle all the stress and conflict and all the jobs: plan a bachelorette party, throw a shower, keep the groom's ring, help the bride with her dress, dance with the best man, give a toast at the reception, hold the bride's bouquet … Maybe I shouldn't have agreed to be in the wedding. Maybe I should back out.

But I can't. The word "no" doesn't exist in my family. The word for "no" in my family is "yes." If Grandma wants me in the wedding, then I'm in the wedding.

Eden and Justin don't have the strength to stand against the hurricane-force wind that is our grandmother. If they need me to stand behind them, then I need a Patron Saint to stand behind *me.* I open my rosary box and pull out the prayer card with Pope Francis's picture. "Dude, you have totally let me down." I put the card back and say a quick prayer to Dominic Savio, Patron Saint of the juvenile delinquents. *Dear Holy Saint Dominic Savio, I just referred to the Pope as a dude. Please forgive me.*

My phone dings with a text message from Mom. Just an hour ago we said good night and our goodbyes because she's leaving early in the morning. She must be texting from Grandma's extra bedroom. Her message says, Don't want to bother you, but I forgot to say the plan for going to church is this: You go to St. George with Grandma, Maggie, and Eden. Luke will go with Will to St. Patrick because he needs a male influence. Love you! xoxo.

I roll my eyes.

Mom must think I'm stupid, but I see what she's doing. She's recruited Uncle Will to keep her secret about Luke not getting First Communion. And that's why she's leaving tomorrow morning instead of Sunday. Mom doesn't want to go to mass. If she does, then Luke would go with us to Grandma's church. Luke couldn't take Communion, and Grandma would want to know why, and then Mom would have to admit he never went through First Communion like every good Catholic boy.

I type, LIAR! My thumb hovers over the send button, but I feel a knot in my throat. I can't do it. I erase everything and send a message that says, Love you, too. But my stomach boils.

There's a knock, and Eden opens the door. "Um . . . can I come in?"

"It's your bedroom. You don't have to knock. I'm the one who should be knocking."

"It's your bedroom, at least for now it's your bedroom, too, so you don't have to knock, either," Eden says.

"Thanks," I say.

She sits on her bed, takes off her glasses, and rubs her eyes. Stress and conflict—just like Google predicted. Here's where I'm supposed to come to the rescue. "Are you okay?"

"This wedding is already a mess. Grandma and Mom wrote up a list of people to invite, and their list is so long. They wrote down the names of second and third cousins I don't even know."

"Did you tell them the list was too big?"

With a sigh heavier than winter wind, Eden flops back on her bed. "Grandma has a way of turning into a train, and you can't stop a train."

"So you didn't tell them."

"No, I didn't tell them. I thought maybe Dad would say something because he doesn't want an expensive reception, but he started adding names. His family is huge! Grandma told him he must be from a colony of bunnies, and he said she should've thought of that before she offered to pay."

"It'll be a nice wedding."

"The only thing that matters is getting married in a church. Mom says every church from the Pacific to the Atlantic will be booked. What if we can't find a church? Will we have to cancel the wedding?"

"You'll find something. If there isn't a church with an opening, well, Grandma will have a church built! Nothing will stop her."

Eden laughs. Even though my answer was ridiculous, I made her feel better.

"I almost forgot. I have something for us." Eden goes to her closet, pulls out a box, and holds it behind her back. "Remember when you were little, and you guys would visit, and everyone would go out for dinner or church bingo, and I'd babysit?"

"Yes."

"Remember what we'd do while everyone was out?"

"Jigsaw puzzles. My favorite was the puzzle with sea creatures."

With a sweep of the arm, Eden shows me the box she's holding. It's a puzzle of the Grand Canyon. I lean forward and squint. "Is that 5,000 pieces?"

"It is!" Eden's eyes are wide with excitement.

"Wow. That's insane!"

"We could start if you want, or not if you don't want."

"Um … okay."

Eden leaves the puzzle next to me and rushes to get her Mom's long craft table. I study the box. The Grand Canyon is splitting the earth into jagged walls of browns and reds with a seamless blue sky. A greenish-blue river twists through the bottom. It's pretty, and it'd be nice to spend a rainy weekend doing a puzzle with Eden, but 5,000 pieces isn't an activity. It's a project. It's a *job*. I see summer flashing before me like a movie. My friends in Holmestrand will play soccer and swim at the lake and have sleepovers while I'm in St. Paul worrying about church availability and how to give a toast. And in between wedding jobs, I'll be putting together the world's hardest puzzle one tiny piece at a time.

Maybe there's a Patron Saint for jigsaw puzzles.

ABOUT BRENT HELZINSKI AND ME

Brent snapped my bra strap. I stepped on his toe.

Brent called me Lip Gloss Queen. I called him Pudge Muffin.

Brent flicked spitballs at me. I stuck chewed-up gum on his desk.

There's going to be a wedding in 54 days

Bam. Bam. Bam. Bam.

The noise drags me from a deep sleep. I open my eyes. Sunlight pours into the room. Eden's bed is made, and her purse is no longer on her desk. She probably left for work.

Bam. Bam. Bam. Bam.

From the window I see Nick in his driveway dribbling a basketball, then shooting a layup. It swirls around the hoop and drops in the basket. Score.

Luke and I have been in St. Paul a week, and I haven't seen Nick since the day with the lawn mower. I wonder if he's stuck in one of those summer programs for kids who are too old for daycare, but with parents who won't leave them home alone.

With the ball tucked under one arm, he *lifts his shirt* and wipes sweat off his face. My face flushes. Then he looks up, straight at the window, and I drop to the floor. Did he see me staring? Maybe he didn't. Maybe the sun created a glare on the window. I probably looked like a shadow. I bet he wasn't even looking at the window. He was staring at a bird or a squirrel or something.

Bam. Bam. Bam. Bam.

It's the sound of *something to do*, something other than playing with Luke at the park or going to the Lego store or talking about the wedding. I'm supposed to go to Grandma's side of the house once I'm awake. I get dressed, pull my hair into a ponytail, and brush my teeth. I have two choices this morning: have breakfast with Luke and Grandma, or go outside.

Outside I go.

I can't just stand in the yard, staring at the sky like some weirdo, so I walk to the mailbox with firm steps and a serious face, like I've got a job to do. An important job. The job of getting the mail. Nick is focused on the hoop.

He dribbles from what would be the free-throw line and takes a shot. It bounces off the backboard. When he catches the ball, he notices me.

"Hi, Mary!"

I give a little wave. "I'm just getting the mail."

"The mail comes late. We must be the last street on the route." He tucks the ball under his arm. "Do you play sports?"

"Soccer. Next year I'll join track, I think."

"Cool."

It's already my turn to ask a question, and my mind is blank. Finally I say, "Do you play basketball?" It's the stupidest question ever, since he's shooting hoops. "In school, I mean. Obviously you're playing basketball right now."

"I'd like to, but my school's huge. You have to be Michael Jordan Junior to make the team. I'm just not good enough."

"My school is so small they'll put you on a team if you have arms."

When he laughs I feel like I scored three points from the middle of the court. He tosses me the ball, and thankfully I catch it. "You know how to play HORSE?"

"Sure."

"I just made a shot from here." He points to a spot about two feet away. "So go ahead and start like you're the second player."

"Okay."

I shoot and miss, so I collect an H. I dribble closer to the net and throw the ball right into the bucket. He can't copy my shot, so he gets an H, too. We each miss a couple of times. It's morning and not yet steamy, but my hands are sweating. I'm sweating everywhere. Finally I throw the ball with a perfect swoosh. It doesn't even touch the backboard.

"Nice," he says, catching the ball. "How long are you staying here?"

"Most of the summer, probably. It depends on when my parents find a house. We're moving to North Dakota."

"Poor you."

"My dad says the people there are really nice."

"It's even colder than here, right?"

"Once you're talking ten below zero, what's another few degrees?" The words are rolling off my tongue. I'm so happy that I haven't gone Eden on him, saying something like, *really it matters not once it's a few degrees below zero in temperature because what's a few more degrees below that temperature?* Immediately I feel bad for making fun of Eden, even if it was only in my head. If there's a Patron Saint for cousins, I'll add him or her to the notebook and say a quick prayer later.

Nick shoots and misses. When I was watching him from the window, I don't think he missed so much. Maybe his hands are sweaty, too. We go back and forth until I'm on R and he's on S.

"You play like a city girl."

"A city girl?"

He says, "You shoot like you could beat a hundred girls for a spot at a huge school."

"Saint Germaine, the Patron Saint of girls from rural areas." It comes out before I think about it, and now I have pulled an Eden. Who talks about Patron Saints? Maybe a couple of nuns having coffee, but not a boy and girl who just met.

"What?"

"Never mind. It's a Catholic thing."

"I'm not Catholic, but of course I know about saints. It's the patron part. What's a Patron Saint?"

"It's nothing, really," I say.

"Patron Saint of girls from rural areas? Is there really such a person?"

"Patron Saints are saints assigned to causes. They're

specialists. They help you with very specific things. They speak to God on your behalf."

"Like how specific?"

"Very. There's Saint Friard for those with a fear of wasps and…hmm…I think Saint Julian is the Patron Saint of carnival workers."

"Carnival workers could probably use their own saint." He tosses me the ball, and I hold it under my arm.

I say, "I personally like Saint Faustina, the Patron Saint of divine mercy because that just sounds cool. Wouldn't Patron Saint of divine mercy be a great name for a band?"

"I like it. What about Mary? Is she like a Patron Saint or a senior saint?"

"Mary the Mother of God?"

"Yeah, Mary. Joseph's baby mama."

My heart squeezes. "Don't say that. It's not right." I might joke about Patron Saints, but Catholics never joke about Mary. Every single month of the year has at least one official feast to honor her, from *Mary the Holy Mother of God* in January to the *Immaculate Conception of the Blessed Virgin Mary* in December. Mary is serious business—holy business.

He runs his hand through his hair and clears his throat. "Sorry. I didn't mean…well, you know."

I don't want to look like a complete Bible-thumper or ruin the moment, so I say, "There's also Saint Drogo, Patron Saint of ugly people."

"Drogo?" He grins. "Sounds like *Lord of the Rings*."

"I know, right?"

Luke runs from the house barefoot and stops at the edge of Uncle Will's lawn. "Mary, you're supposed to come inside for breakfast."

"In a minute."

"Grandma said if you say 'in a minute' then I'm supposed to say 'right now.'"

I roll my eyes and toss the ball to Nick. "I've got to go."

As Luke and I walk toward the house, Nick calls out, "You don't need any help from Drogo in case you were wondering."

Drogo, the Patron Saint of ugly people. I don't need help from him. Is that what he said? I'm pretty sure that's what he said. I don't turn around. I act like I haven't heard him even though his words replay in my head over and over and over.

There's going to be a wedding in 45 days

As soon as I get to the kitchen Sunday morning, I know there's going to be trouble because Uncle Will is coughing and blowing his nose. He rubs his temples and says, "I've got the mother of all headaches. No church for me."

My heart pounds. He absolutely has to take Luke to church, otherwise the secret will blow up. Grandma will freak out, and Mom will freak out about Grandma freaking out. It'll be emotional dominoes.

I whisper, "Uncle Will, what about Luke?"

"He can go to church with you." His eyes widen as he remembers what he's supposed to do and why. He leans against the counter and shakes his head. "Shoot. I forgot about the…um…situation with Luke. I guess I better go. I don't want Maggie finding out."

Aunt Maggie is a tattletale. When I won the youth group award, she sent me an e-mail to say congratulations. I wrote back something random, like "maybe we'll have a pizza party," and within five minutes Grandma called Mom to scold her for not inviting the family to my party. That's how fast the family phone tree works!

Uncle Will coughs so hard his face turns purple, and he grabs the refrigerator handle for support.

"What's wrong?" Aunt Maggie comes into the kitchen and puts her hand on Uncle Will's forehead. "I can hear you from the upstairs bathroom. Hmm. I think you have a fever."

"I'll take some aspirin and nap when I get home."

"You will not spread germs to an entire congregation. God will understand. Go to bed."

"I'm fine. Don't fuss over me."

"Are you crazy? You've got no business being around old people and babies. Go to bed. I'll bring up some aspirin and juice." She turns to me. "You better hurry, Mary. Grandma likes to get a good seat."

I look at Uncle Will with wide eyes. He sighs and pats

me on the shoulder. "It is what it is, Mary." He coughs his way upstairs to his bedroom with Aunt Maggie trailing behind him.

It is what it is?

If that's an example of Irish wisdom, then I'm on Grandma's side of their battle. I can't imagine saying those words. *Mary, your room is a mess... Well, Dad, it is what it is.*

Luke enters from Grandma's side of the house. He's wearing his tan church pants, and his hair is slicked back. "Mary, this is the best Sunday ever! You know why?"

"Why?"

"It's doughnut day at Uncle Will's church. Too bad for you. I get doughnuts and you don't." He immediately looks guilty for his singsong teasing. "It's okay. I'll bring one back for you."

I try to sound like I've got everything under control. "Change in plans, buddy. Uncle Will is sick, so you're coming to church with us." I call him buddy only when he's really down. It sounds like I'm talking to a dog, but he seems to like it.

He shuffles closer to me. "What am I supposed to do?"

"Let me think about it. I'll figure it out."

"Mom said I *have to* go with Uncle Will." His voice turns to a whisper. "I *have to* because Grandma doesn't need to know everything right now and it's not a lie because we are going to tell her but we're going to tell her later."

I can handle being stuck between Mom and Grandma— I've got loads of practice—but it's wrong that Luke's in the middle of this mess. He's eight years old. He only sees the surface of problems, not the layers upon layers underneath. I try out Uncle Will's words because I can't think of anything else. "It is what it is, Luke."

"What's that supposed to mean?"

I shrug, but I'm thinking, *It means we're on our own.*

Luke wiggles through the procession and greetings at St. George. He's waiting for me to figure out what he's supposed to do. I think about going directly to God, but then I remember John Danner and all the people who really, truly need Him. Why haven't I looked for a Patron Saint of Communion? This situation calls for an expert. The best I've got is Saint Jude Thaddaeus, Patron Saint of lost causes.

Dear Holy Saint Jude, I wish I'd given you some warning, but I thought the adults had this figured out. I need an idea, and I need it in five minutes.

I look at Eden, who's watching Father Owens with her

hands folded on her lap. I wonder what she'd do. She's close to Grandma. Maybe she'd throw her mom under the bus and tell Grandma the truth. Aunt Maggie wouldn't even get mad at Eden for blowing it, because everyone worries about Eden. Aunt Maggie and Grandma do everything for her—mostly Grandma, since she's retired—because when Eden's anxiety gets bad, she gets depressed and sick.

Father Owens begins the preparation of Communion by praying over it. The congregation stands. In the Catholic church, mass is Sunday morning exercise. Stand, sit, kneel, sit, kneel, stand, sit. I guess it keeps people from falling asleep. But I'm not at risk of falling asleep, I'm thinking of plans. Luke could pretend to be sick and go to the bathroom, except he's a terrible faker. Grandma won't buy it, especially since he's been acting normal all morning. I could pretend to be sick, get Grandma to follow me to the bathroom, and then Luke could stay in the pew during Communion. But Grandma probably wouldn't follow me until *after* Communion. You don't miss Communion just because a kid's puking.

Father Owens leads the congregation with his booming voice. "May the Lord accept the sacrifice at your hands, for the praise and glory of his name, for our good and the good of all the Church."

It's getting close.

Father Owens holds the wine toward Heaven and prays. "Take this, all of you, and drink from it, for this is the cup of my blood, the blood of the new and everlasting covenant, which will be poured out for you and for many, so sins will be forgiven."

We're almost out of time. I whisper to Luke, "You're going to have to take Communion. There's no way around it."

"Can't I put it in my pocket or something?" Luke's voice cuts through the prayer.

Grandma frowns and shushes him. When she's facing Father again, I nudge Luke and whisper. "Trust me. You cannot put it in your pocket. That's the worst thing you could do. You have to eat it."

His eyes open to me, big and blue and sweet. "The Pope says I'm not supposed to."

I'm glad Luke doesn't know the whole deal about Catholic Communion. The Pope is the least of his problems! In our church, when the priest blesses the wafer and the wine, he's basically turning it into the Body and Blood of Christ. Not basically. Wrong word. *Literally*. He's literally turning the wafer and wine into Christ's Body and Blood. Some people think it's symbolic, but it's not. I pay attention in religion class. It's called "transubstantiation," which I can't even pronounce, and it's a miraculous thing that happens, even though the wafer and wine still look exactly like the wafer and wine when the priest is done. We're not supposed to think it's gross because Jesus wanted it this way.

But I'm sure God will forgive a little kid for taking Communion too soon, as long as the kid is doing it *right*. Putting the actual body of Christ in his pocket is definitely doing it wrong. As everyone lines up for Communion, Luke grabs my hand, and we follow Aunt Maggie, Eden, and Grandma. He keeps looking at me, waiting for me to think of something smarter. I stare ahead and act like I know what I'm doing.

When we get to Father Owens, Luke holds out his hand, and Father places the wafer in his palm saying, "Body of Christ." Luke doesn't say amen. He shifts to the side and waits for me to get my wafer.

"Body of Christ." Father Owens puts the wafer in my palm, and I put it in my mouth and say, "Amen."

The Body of Christ tastes like cardboard. The Communion bakers should flavor it with cinnamon and sugar. How hard could it be to add a few sprinkles? I doubt Jesus would mind. I keep the wafer on my tongue and wait for it to dissolve, because if you press it on the roof of your mouth, it turns to glue and you can't get it off unless you scrape with your finger. You don't chew the Body of Christ.

Luke and I walk past Father Owens's helper, who has tiny plastic cups filled with the wine. Grandma doesn't mind if we skip this part because it's actually alcohol. I mean, the priest's blessing turns the alcohol in the cups into Jesus's Blood. Transubstantiation, remember? But somehow it's also still alcohol.

My family returns to our pew and kneels, except for Luke, who's sitting on the edge of the pew still holding the wafer. Grandma leans across me and whispers, "Lucas Matthew, put that in your mouth right now."

Luke's hand shakes as he puts the wafer on the tip of his tongue, but then he freezes. His tongue hangs out like a panting dog.

"What is wrong with you? Act like a big boy!" Grandma says.

He sucks his tongue and the wafer into his mouth. He looks at me with big eyes, like he's waiting for something terrible to happen. I whisper, "It's okay. I researched it just in case you couldn't get out of it."

When Grandma returns to prayer, Luke gags a little

and then jumps up and runs down the aisle toward the door. I did not see that coming!

I have to do something. I can't have Luke wandering around the parking lot. I tap Grandma's shoulder and say, "Luke left because he's missing Dad. I'll go talk to him."

She nods. Grandma wouldn't leave her pew during post-Communion prayer unless the church was on fire. I hustle outside and find Luke sitting on the curb next to Aunt Maggie's minivan.

"Are you okay, buddy?"

There's a tear on his thick eyelashes. He shrugs and holds out his hand to show me the wafer, which is now a spit-drenched glob. "I couldn't swallow it because it's against Catholic law, and what if the Pope finds out?"

I sit next to him. "You get a pass because you're eight."

He sticks his hand with the wafer under my chin. "You eat it. You're allowed. It's good for you because it's like being blessed twice."

"That's disgusting! I'm not going to take your chewed-up clump of grossness and eat it."

Luke frowns in concentration. "God loves everyone, right? All people, even animals?"

"Yes."

"Then we can feed it to a squirrel."

"Absolutely not."

"A bird?"

"No way. Just let me think."

His lower lip goes out, and he puts his hand on his lap and stares at the wafer. Then, in a swift move, he smears the goop on my lap and runs back to the church as fast as his legs will pump.

"Luke!"

I want to tackle him, but he's too fast, and the Body of Christ is stuck to my sundress.

"Luke!" He's already inside the church. I scrape off the wafer and hold it in my palm. Luke has a grand plan, and it involves getting me to eat the wafer, but I can't. If I put that spit-covered wafer in my mouth, I will puke, and it's definitely bad to throw up Jesus.

This is stupid. Our church has seven Holy Sacraments. *Seven.* That's not much. One is when you're born and one is when you die and one is if you become a priest, so that really only leaves four. Only *two* of those four are when you're really young—Confession and Communion. Mom managed to get Luke through Confession, but Communion has been an epic fail. The way I see it, she's got a 50 percent failure rate in the job of Catholic parenting.

Why am I the one sitting in a parking lot with the

Body of Christ on my dress? It should be Mom, because it's her truth-stretch; not mine! I take a few deep breaths to calm down. I'm so mad I'm probably breaking the Commandment about honoring parents. I don't need a Communion sin *and* a broken Commandment on my shoulders.

The breathing calms me down until I see Grandma, Luke, Eden, and Aunt Maggie on their way to the van. Luke is holding Grandma's hand and smiling like there's nothing wrong in the world. As I put the Body of Christ in the pocket of my sundress, I wish Brent's face were in front of me to punch. That horrible thought makes me shiver. I'm an award-winning nice girl, and I can't lose control like that again.

Ever.

As soon as we get home, I fly up the stairs and get out my laptop. I type *Patron Saint of Communion* and click on the first search result, the Blessed Imelda, and speed-read.

Most saints are saints because they had hard lives. You don't get to be a saint by winning the lottery and driving your new convertible to the beach. Saint Germaine Cousin was abused by her horrible stepmother. Saint Helen's husband divorced her and ran off with another woman. Saint Rene Goupil was tortured for being Christian. Easy lives don't make saints.

But Blessed Imelda's story is the worst I've ever read.

Hundreds of years ago, Imelda was a little girl so devout she dreamed of being a nun. She was desperate to receive her First Communion, but the priest wouldn't allow it because she was too young. One day, she continued to kneel at mass even though it was time to stand. She wanted her First Communion. A beautiful light appeared above Imelda. Everyone could see it. The priest knew the light was a miracle, so he felt it was his calling to give her Communion. Imelda's prayers were about to come true! When she accepted the Communion wafer, she fell into a state of complete joy.

And then she died.

Everyone believed Imelda died from *joy*. They also believed she was lucky because God loved her so much He took her home to Heaven. If that's how God shows His love, I don't want Him to love me that much. Not yet.

Seriously, there's no way she died from joy. I'd bet anything she was choking on her Communion wafer and jumping around and grabbing her throat, and all those adults stood around smiling at each other, not even thinking about the Heimlich maneuver. *Check out little Imelda. She's fallen into a state of joy.*

Poor Imelda!

Anyway, I need her help. I write her name in the notebook, add a star, and pray.

Dear Holy Blessed Imelda, I've got a Communion problem on my hands. It's not as bad as choking to death on the wafer, but it's close. I've got a half-chewed piece of Communion and I don't know what to do with it. Please help me fix this.

With my eyes closed and my hands pressed together, I try to hear or think or feel Blessed Imelda's answer. Nothing. Not a single movement, sound, thought, feeling. When I finally open my eyes and look at the clock, it says I've been sitting like that for twenty minutes. That's almost as long as it takes to say the rosary.

I scrape the wafer from my pocket and take my rosary box from the nightstand. The box is the holiest place to store the Body of Christ until Blessed Imelda speaks to me. I gently tuck the wafer next to the rosary. I cover it with the Pope Francis prayer card. I don't want Eden to open the box and find it, and I can't have Luke looking for it and feeding it to a bird. I take my suitcase from the closet and zip the box inside. There's a small padlock and key attached to the suitcase with a piece of plastic. It's one of those locks that prevents someone from unzipping the suitcase. With a tug, I pull the lock and key from the plastic and lock the zipper. Then I hide the key in my underwear drawer.

Dear Holy Blessed Imelda, Just think about it and get back to me, okay?

ABOUT BRENT HELZINSKI AND ME

BRENT HELZINSKI WAS INVITED TO RYAN DORMAN'S Halloween party. The whole class was invited, and I know that's the only reason Brent got an invitation. Ryan's parents probably made him add Brent to the list. And Ryan was probably afraid Brent would beat him up if he left him out.

Who'd invite Brent Helzinski to anything?

After that party, I needed Saint Michael the Archangel, Patron Saint for those going into battle. Or maybe Gertrude of Nevilles, Patron Saint for protection from rats.

Chapter Eleven

There's going to be a wedding in **42** days

It's exactly nine in the morning when I hear a swooshing and clacking noise. I press my pillow against my ears to muffle the sound until I realize it's coming from Nick's driveway. Suddenly I'm awake.

I get up and stand sideways behind Eden's lamp, so I can see clearly down to his driveway without him seeing me. Nick is on a skateboard near the street. He pushes his right foot carefully against the cement, then strikes an uneasy balance on the board. His first push takes him maybe two feet, so he repeats the process.

After the Communion mess, I could use some laughs. I get dressed and head outside. Nick smiles when he sees me walking across the yard. He pushes down on the end of the skateboard with his foot. The back side flips up, and he catches it with his right hand.

"So you're a basketball champ and a skateboarder."

"Watch this." He puts the skateboard down, steps on it, and wobbles as the board clunks ahead a few feet. "That's the best I can do. Skateboarders would take me down if I called myself one of them."

"There's a guy in my old neighborhood who could do these crazy jumps on his board. My mom would freak out because he never wore a helmet."

"My mom got this at a garage sale, and technically I'm supposed to wear my bike helmet, but I'm not even going grandmother speed yet." Nick's bangs fall across his forehead, so he sweeps them aside. He has cute hair and a cute smile and cute eyes. He is bursting with cute. "Want to try it?"

"Sure." I stand on the skateboard, bend my knee, and push off. I forget to put my other foot on the board and nearly tip over. The board flies across the driveway, and I jump off before it crashes into the garage door.

"Maybe we should get a helmet." Nick laughs.

"And kneepads."

"And elbow pads."

"A full suit of body armor."

We stand there, sort of looking at the ground, thinking of what to say next. A neighbor starts a lawn mower, and the dog across the street barks at a squirrel. I start talking about the dog just as Nick starts saying something about the lawn mower. Then we both stop talking and wait for the other to finish.

Finally Nick says, "You go first."

I freeze. For the life of me, I can't remember what I was going to say. I feel my face turn Eden-red. "No, you go."

Nick trips over his words. "I was thinking about the lawn and mowing the lawn, which I should do tomorrow, maybe. But, anyway, should I get my basketball?"

Nick's stumbling gives me time to pull myself together. I say, "No, let's keep doing this. I refuse to be defeated by a skateboard."

We take turns on the skateboard until we're stable. Then we take it to the sidewalk so we can time each other skateboarding from the street corner to Nick's house. When I make the run in an impressive five seconds, I try to pop up the skateboard with my foot and catch it like Nick, but it snaps faster than I expect and bangs my knee. Not cool.

Nick says, "I'll laugh if you're not hurt."

My knee throbs, but it is pretty funny, so we crack up.

Eden comes out of the house wearing her laundry uniform. I call out a hello. She gives a little wave, but she keeps her eyes on the ground like she's watching for land mines. She starts her car and drives away.

"Is that your cousin?" Nick asks.

"Yeah. Her name is Eden."

"I've never heard of anyone being named Eden."

"My Uncle Will really liked the name Eve, but my grandma didn't like it because Eve ruined the Garden of Eden, and if it weren't for Eve, we'd all be living in paradise."

"Um . . . do you believe that?"

"I believe Eden's an unusual name for an unusual person."

Nick nods. "Yeah, it's a good name."

"She's getting married, and the whole thing is weird. She wants it small, but my grandma basically wants a pageant. I'm the junior bridesmaid."

"I was a ring bearer in my cousin's wedding when I was five," Nick says. "I remember I carried around this stupid red pillow and the ring was tied to it with a ribbon. Isn't it crazy to put an expensive ring on a pillow and trust a kindergartner to hang on to it?"

"Did you lose the ring?"

"No, but I had a tantrum because I didn't want my picture taken. My mom took me in the hall and promised if I was good for the whole day we'd stay overnight at a waterpark."

"Nice bribe."

"Well, I thought I could do better. So I asked her for SpongeBob socks instead. I really, really wanted SpongeBob socks for some reason."

I laugh and Nick, grinning, says, "I'm totally serious."

"Mary Margaret Miller!" Grandma yells from her front door. "What are you doing?" She's so loud Nick actually backs away.

"Nothing," I say. "Just skateboarding."

"Get away from that thing. You'll break your arm and ruin the wedding."

Nick raises his eyebrows, and I shrug, like *What can you do?*

She yells, "Come inside and have breakfast. I made cinnamon rolls."

I push my foot on the skateboard's tip. This time I catch the board when it flips, and I hand it to Nick. "See you later."

"Okay."

"Don't dilly dally!" Grandma yells.

"Dilly dally?" Nick laughs. "You better get going, you rapscallion."

"What's a rapscallion?"

"I heard it in an old black-and-white movie."

"Mary!"

I say, "That's her last-warning voice. I better go."

"See you later, rapscallion."

I hold back giggles so Grandma doesn't make me tell her what's so funny.

Chapter Twelve

There's going to be a wedding in 40 days

"AN AUGUST WEDDING? AND YOU JUST *STARTED* LOOKING for dresses?" The voice of shock comes from a sales lady with a nametag that says *Paula T., Wedding Consultant*.

Grandma gets haughty. "The reason for the short timeline isn't inappropriate. The groom is starting graduate school in another state, so they're moving. He's going to be a biomedical researcher." Grandma makes biomedical researcher sound like the most important thing a person could do, definitely more important than being a wedding consultant.

"I'm afraid the selection I can offer you—that *any* store could offer you—is very limited. Dresses take months to order. You'll have to find something that fits on the rack."

Eden realizes she, as the bride, is expected to answer. She blushes and looks at her feet and says, "We're understanding."

"Have a look at the racks. We can always alter a dress if it's a close fit. I'll be happy to open a dressing suite for you." Paula T. leaves us to help another bridal party, a party that probably planned way better than us.

Grandma pats Eden's back. "Don't worry. We'll find the world's most beautiful dress for the world's most beautiful bride."

"Maybe we should wait for the weekend when Aunt Maggie can come with us," I say.

Grandma sighs. "She's working overtime all week, and there's just no time. We have to dig in and find something beautiful. Luke, do not wander off."

"Is this going to take long?" Luke asks.

"As long as it needs to, and there will be no complaining from you." Her voice is stern, but she hugs him. "Besides, we need your opinion."

The store is divided into wedding dresses, bridesmaid dresses, and racks of mom-and-grandma dresses, the kind with sequined jackets that hide bulging tummies.

Grandma shows me a dress from the bridesmaid section. It's hunter green with a fat bow on the butt. She must know that color died before I was born. When I don't gush over the hunter green, Grandma says, "Well, it's not like we don't have choices. Look at all these dresses! Look at the colors! I think a rainbow melted in this store!"

I wish she'd wander off so we can look without her hovering.

Luke is already bored. "This would go faster if you look at the Grandma dresses and Mary looks at the bridesmaid dresses and Eden looks at the bride dresses."

"Okay," Grandma says. "But you stay next to me."

Paula T. swoops in just as Grandma swoops out. "What are you thinking for the bridal party? Any particular color or style?"

Eden says, "Colors? I haven't thought of colors, or thought of styles, at this particular point in time." Eden points to me. "She's the junior bridesmaid." Normally I'd tell her I'll wear whatever she wants me to wear, but I'm pretty sure she wants me to take charge. She's blushing and chewing on her thumbnail.

I think about how a grown-up bridesmaid would answer and say, "What do you suggest?"

"It used to be a summer wedding meant pastel, but it's

not that way anymore," Paula T. says. "I've sold brown dresses for summer. Brown! Certainly it'll be warm, so you'll want short sleeves or spaghetti straps or something strapless. Blue would be lovely with the rich brown tones in your hair. You have gorgeous hair. I'd suggest leaving it down."

I say, "I like blue."

Eden nods. "Blue is good."

"Now we have a place to start. Also, if you find a dress, but you don't like the color, we can always order—oh wait, you're the ones with the quickie wedding." She sighs. "Follow me, girls."

She takes us to a rack of dresses in various shades of blue, more shades than I knew existed. Light blue and dark blue. Blue muddled with greens and purples. Powder blue and iridescent blue. Paula T. pats me on the back and leaves.

"It doesn't matter to me, Mary," Eden says. "You should pick what you like. Just please don't make it expensive, no matter what Grandma says."

"Okay."

Eden heads toward the bridal gowns, but something in the rack of pink dresses catches her eye. She shifts dresses back and forth and pulls out one of the gowns. Her face brightens. The dress is soft pink and full of lace and ribbons and pearls and sparkles. She carries it to a large mirror and holds the dress against her body.

"Mary, would it be crazy if I wore this dress? I thought I didn't care about dresses, but since I'm here and I'm getting one, well, I like it. I think I love it, actually."

Relief runs from my fingers to my toes. It's not for *me*. "It looks so nice against your hair. It really accentuates the blond tones." I have no idea where I got those words, but it sounds like something Paula T. would say.

"This is it." Eden grins. "This is the one. I think it will fit."

"Try it on. I want to see it."

Grandma comes from nowhere and touches the fabric. "How lovely! Mary, this is perfect for a young bridesmaid."

"Not for me," I say. "For Eden. She wants this dress for herself."

Grandma laughs. "It's beautiful, but brides wear white."

"Why?" Luke asks.

"They just do."

"But why?"

"If she wears a dress like this people will think it's her second marriage. Divorced women who are getting remarried wear colors. Eden has to wear white." Grandma's voice is firm. "Eden, your mother should be on her lunch break, so let's have her weigh in on this."

"You don't have to call Mom." Eden says, but buttons have already been pushed and in seconds, Aunt Maggie is on the screen of Grandma's phone, and they're chattering about wedding dresses with the speaker at full volume.

Paula T., stationed at the register, stretches her head like an ostrich to watch, and an entire bridal party starts to circle. Grandma uses the phone to show Aunt Maggie the pink dress. She turns the phone so Aunt Maggie is looking at Eden and me. Aunt Maggie says, "Eden, you simply cannot wear pink. It's not appropriate."

"How about for Mary?" Grandma shouts so Aunt Maggie can hear.

"I think it's fine for a bridesmaid," Aunt Maggie says.

One of the shoppers studies Eden and says, "They're doing you a favor. Unless you get highlights, this dress will not go with your hair."

A woman with purple eye shadow says, "You have strong shoulders. You should wear strapless."

Her friend touches the dress. "This looks more like a ball gown. It's very old-fashioned."

"Too princess-y." An older woman, probably a mom, nods.

There's disagreement, though, as an even older woman, probably a grandma, says, "Gorgeous. Absolutely stunning."

More brides and bridesmaids shuffle over, and their comments start rolling together. Beads, trains, lace, veils, pearls, shoes. Then there are words I've never heard—tulle overskirt, illusion sleeves, chiffon, sheath, bodice. That's followed by a discussion of the various shades of white—champagne, cream, ivory, candlelight, rum, eggshell, ecru.

I'm so embarrassed I want to crawl under the dress with the biggest skirt and hide, and I'm pretty sure Eden wants to join me. Grandma says, "Well, girls, as long as we have a crowd we should model some of these dresses."

Eden shakes her head no, and I see the sweat beads forming on her forehead. Google said my job is to help the bride handle stress and conflict, and this definitely qualifies as stress and conflict for Eden. I take the princess dress from Grandma and say, "I'll try on this one, but the bride shouldn't have to model. It's bad luck, right?"

Eden's shoulders relax, and she gives me a half smile. A score for the junior bridesmaid!

Ten minutes later, half of the shoppers are crammed into the dressing suite, and I'm modeling the princess dress. There are gasps, and I'm not sure they're all wow-that's-beautiful gasps. I think some gasps are more like *oh my*

God because the princess dress looks like a craft store exploded on cotton candy. It has everything: pearls and ribbons and sparkles and lace and a bow and a large, gathered skirt. I'm not wearing this dress—this dress is wearing *me*.

I swallow my horror and embarrassment by pretending it's a Halloween costume, and I'm just trick-or-treating. In a bridal shop. In June. In front of women who have purses instead of bags of candy.

Grandma turns to Eden and, as if it matters, she asks, "What do you think?"

Eden shrugs. "Nice."

Paula T. nods, and the slur of words from the brides and their maids begins again: lavish, darling, sweet, lovely, ornate. I catch a whisper from the woman in the corner. "Over the top," she says to her friend.

And then this comes from Luke. "Cinderella! Mary looks like Cinderella."

Luke nailed it. This dress is Cinderella meets Belle meets Sleeping Beauty. Throw in an apple and you'd have Snow White, too. Paula T. pulls at the dress here and there and announces the fit is close enough to alter. She measures me up and down and all around and sends the dress to the back room for alteration.

Finally, everyone scatters, and Grandma leads us to

the racks of white gowns and starts sorting until Eden rubs her forehead. "I just got the worst headache." Grandma touches her face, checking for a fever. She sighs, puts her arm around Eden, and says, "I guess we'll have to come back. There's no time to waste, so I'll insist they give us another appointment tomorrow."

Luke stomps his foot. "We have to do this again tomorrow?! I'd rather watch a documentary on toothpicks." I don't know where Luke picked up that line, but he uses it every time he has to do something he doesn't like, and he usually gets a huge laugh, even from me. But not this time. I'm feeling bad about wearing the dress Eden wants for herself, the only thing she's asked for during all the wedding talk. In this moment, even toothpick documentaries aren't funny.

ABOUT BRENT HELZINSKI AND ME

BRENT HELZINSKI IS PROBABLY PLOTTING REVENGE ALL
the way from Holmestrand.

Fine by me. I don't even care.

Chapter Thirteen

There's going to be a wedding in 38 days

JESSICA ISN'T ONLINE, SO I TYPE HER AN E-MAIL ABOUT the princess dress and the "party" Grandma's planned for tonight.

> Grandma invited her church friends to an
> invitation-writing party, which is really just a
> group of us stuffing wedding invitations into
> envelopes. Grandma said we can call it a party
> because she's going to have punch and cake.

My phone rings. I look around Eden's bedroom, but I

don't see it, so I flip the blankets on my bed. Sure enough, my phone is under the sheet.

It's Mom.

My thumb hovers over the "talk" button. My stomach boils while I stare at the words "Mom calling" and listen to it ring and ring. I tell myself to answer the call, but I don't. I don't want to talk to her. As the call rolls into voicemail, Grandma yells from downstairs, "Mary! We need your help!"

"Just a minute."

"Young lady, if I needed you in a minute, I would have waited a minute to call you."

"I'm coming!"

Downstairs, Aunt Maggie and Eden are sitting at the dining room table with Grandma's friends. Grandma introduces them. "Elaine, Connie, and Beth reporting for duty!" Then she sets a laptop at the end of the table by an empty chair.

"I thought I'd get Bernie to join us."

"Mom doesn't have wireless at the motel," I say.

"There was an opening at another motel across town, so they switched," Aunt Maggie says. "But I don't think Bernie wants to watch us write invitations."

Grandma waves, like she's brushing the words out of the air. Mom appears on the screen. "Hi everyone! Perfect timing. I just tried calling Mary." I smile and wave at the screen. I feel guilty for not answering the call, but I'm also mad about Communion. Grandma explains the plan for the night and puts stacks of envelopes in front of each of us along with photocopied pages from her address book. "Take your time. Use your most beautiful handwriting."

"Sounds like you've got a long evening ahead of you. I should probably let you go so I don't distract you," Mom says. "Wish I could be there."

"You are here!" Grandma pats the laptop like it's Mom's head. "Family is never a distraction."

I say, "We could type these into a label program, print them, and stick them on the envelopes. Wouldn't that be easier and neater?"

Grandma and her friends laugh. Grandma says, "Right! How about we just send text messages with an invitation. L-O-L!"

"Grandma likes to do things the old-fashioned way," Aunt Maggie says. "And we appreciate it, don't we Eden?"

Eden blushes. "Yes, it's appreciated by me certainly."

"You kids these days don't practice your cursive, so I'm going to show you what beautiful handwriting looks like." Grandma slowly writes on an envelope and puts it in front of me. "See how pretty it is and how personal it looks?"

Mr. and Mrs. George Neustrand
1400 West Ridge Road
Holton, Minnesota 59023

I nod. "Yes, Grandma, that's beautiful."

"When I was a little girl, penmanship mattered. This would have earned me an A." Grandma hands me a piece of scrap paper. "Mary, practice on this first."

Luke comes from the kitchen with a glass of milk. Peanut butter is smeared above his lip like a mustache. He lifts his shirt and wipes milk from his chin. "What about me? Don't I get to help? Hi, Mom!"

"Hi, sweetie!"

"Sure, honey," Aunt Maggie says, although Grandma raises an eyebrow. "You can put on the stamps."

"But they have to be perfectly straight!" Grandma says. "And you can't touch anything until you change your shirt and wash your face and hands."

Luke heads over to Grandma's side of the house for a clean shirt. I tell her, "He'll be bored after three stamps."

"It's just an envelope with a stamp being stuck on it," Eden says. "He can't make a mistake with it, I don't think."

Grandma snorts. "Just a stamp? And I suppose this is *just* a wedding?"

"Of course not," Aunt Maggie says. "Quality control is important."

Everyone stops talking because we're concentrating. Grandma's friends are writing so slowly I can barely see their fingers move. I hardly ever write in cursive. I practice writing *Mr. and Mrs. Richard R. Collins* on the scrap paper.

Mom says, "You're starting to freeze up. I think I'm losing the connection."

Stretch goes the rubber band! Under my breath I say, "Blasted Internet!"

And the screen goes blank.

Chapter Fourteen

There's going to be a wedding
in 33 days

EDEN AND I ARE HUNCHED OVER THE PUZZLE FOR THE third night in a row. She's completed an entire corner while I've done nothing but sort pieces into color groups. I can't stop thinking about Blessed Imelda and the chewed-up Communion wafer hidden in my rosary box. I almost showed it to Eden yesterday. She knows about Catholic rules and what Grandma is like and what Mom is like. But my job is to help with Eden's stress and conflict, not to heap layers on her. So I keep it inside.

I press a couple of pieces together, but they don't fit. The pieces are the same shade of sky blue with the same pattern, and they will not snap together. Eden, though, is gently pressing together piece after piece, forming a beige ribbon that ripples through the red stone.

"How did you get so good?"

"I just study things," Eden says. "I don't say much, but I pay attention."

"Oh."

"You'd be surprised what you notice when you're invisible. Watch Grandma, for instance. She talks all the time, and that's what most people notice. They hear but they don't see. She always gives a quick tug on her right ear when she's frustrated. Always her right ear. The more frustrated she is, the more she does it. She also tips her head when she smiles. Just a little and always to the left."

"Interesting. What do you notice about me?"

"You keep everything inside. You always say 'oh' or 'okay' or 'sure.' You don't ever really respond to things people say."

My back feels stiff. "You don't respond much, either."

"I do take medication for social anxiety disorder, Mary."

"I talk! I talked to customers all the time at the store. And I have a bunch of friends."

Eden squints at the pieces in front of her, looking for subtle difference in color. I think I hurt her feelings. "I don't mean you don't have friends." I say, "That's not what I meant. I'm sure you have friends. I know you do."

"I have a friend from the hospital laundry. Her name is Emma. She's thirty and she has two kids, but she's always been nice to me."

"Of course she is. Why wouldn't she be?"

"People weren't nice in school. I was chubby in elementary school, and kids called me the Garden of Eatin'."

"That's terrible."

"In junior high girls used to stick maxi pads to my back."

I say, "This guy Brent calls me 'Scary Mary' and 'Hairy Mary.'"

"Brent? I had a tormentor named Brent, too. He put a mouse in my locker, and it shredded my English notebook, but I didn't want to tell my teacher because she'd make a big deal out of it. Things would get worse instead of better. I lost all the notes for my big research paper, and I barely passed the class." Her voice is calm, like she's reporting financial news. I know she didn't have many friends, and I know about her anxiety disorder, but I didn't know people were flat-out mean to her.

Eden sighs. "It gets easier in high school. By senior year, people grow out of their meanness, mostly. Then they ignored me, and that made everything easier."

I'm sad that being ignored was an improvement for Eden. Once I overheard Aunt Maggie say how much she worries because Eden's a loner and kids don't appreciate her thoughtfulness. Then Grandma chimed in that Eden had family, and that's all people need.

"I hear you're spending a lot of time with the neighbor kid." Eden's voice has a hint of teasing.

"Not really."

She raises her eyebrows. "Grandma looks out the window a lot."

I groan and drop my face into my hands as Eden laughs. "Our grandmother is crazy!"

Eden says, "I know, but it's good crazy. Mostly it's good crazy. You know, there's good crazy, and there's bad crazy."

"Did she go on any other dates with you and Justin? Because one date is good crazy. Any more than that is bad crazy."

"Sometimes we invite her because she's lonely. She can be really fun, and Justin is so sweet to her. You know what? She wants us to play laser tag with her."

"You are not serious."

"I am completely serious." She giggles. "Imagine her dressed in black with goggles over her silver hair."

We completely crack up. I want to ask more about

Justin. I almost ask if she kisses Justin, but DUH, of course she does. Still I wonder if she kissed him or if he kissed her or if they kissed at the exact same time, but I know she'll turn eight shades of purple if I bring it up. She'll say it's time for bed, and the night will end.

And I don't want it to end, because talking with Eden is awesome, even if it involves 5,000 puzzle pieces.

ABOUT BRENT HELZINSKI AND ME

I'D RATHER THINK ABOUT JESUS'S DISAPPOINTMENT WITH me for storing His Body in a rosary box than think about Brent Helzinski.

I am *done* thinking about Brent Helzinski.

Chapter Fifteen

There's going to be a wedding in **29** days

"Mary, I need help." Eden shuffles through her room wearing a robe, opens the closet, and freezes. "I don't have anything to wear."

We're meeting Justin's parents at an Italian restaurant where Aunt Maggie booked a private room. I'm wearing my blue sundress with a flowing skirt, and Grandma let me use mascara. She says thick, dark eyelashes make my brown eyes look dramatic. While Eden stares into her closet, I peek out the window to see if Nick's outside. He's not.

Eden says, "I thought I didn't care about clothes, and I don't, but suddenly I do. What's wrong with me? Justin says his parents don't care about things like fancy clothes. Am I becoming a bridezilla?"

"You're not a bridezilla, but you're going to make us late. Just pick out something and then do your hair."

"My hair doesn't look done?" Eden turns her head from side to side so I can get a full view. "I tried to fluff it out. I followed directions from a bridal magazine Grandma bought me."

"It looks like your hair got caught in a ceiling fan," Luke says from the doorway.

How'd he get to Eden's room without me hearing the squeaky floorboards in the hall? That kid should be a spy.

"Luke doesn't know what he's talking about. You're beautiful. I just need to smooth it down a bit." I use my palm to tame the fluffiest sections of her hair. "Get out of here, Luke. We're busy."

"Grandma says Aunt Maggie and Uncle Will are going to meet us at the restaurant and you're already five minutes late and she'll give you five more minutes because the bride can be fashionably late but anything more than ten minutes is not fashionable. It's just rude."

Eden sits on the bed and sighs. "I can't do this. I can't. There has to be another way."

"What's wrong with your eyes, Mary?" Luke squints. "Your eyelashes are clumpy."

"Go!" I point at the door, and he stomps down the hall. This time I hear the floorboards.

I remember the job of a bridesmaid. *Emotional support during conflict and stress.*

"I'll find something for you to wear. Want to lay down for a few minutes?"

"I can't. My hair will get flat."

Eden's closet is filled with plain cotton shirts and, I swear, about a dozen pairs of khaki pants. There's one dress, but it's black with long sleeves. She wore it to our great uncle's funeral. Toward the back is a collection of skorts, which tells me Grandma found a sale. Finally I see a real skirt. It's a simple black wrap-around, and it'll go with anything.

"Here." I hold out the black wrap-around skirt and a frilly tank top. "These look perfect together."

"I'm serious, Mary. I can't do this. I can't. There has to be another way." She nervously twists the belt from her robe around her hand.

"This is the cutest outfit ever." I nearly squeak with enthusiasm. "Why haven't I seen you in this? It'll go great with your fluffy hair."

"I mean the wedding! I don't think I can do a wedding. It's too much."

"Oh." I say a quick prayer: *Dear Holy Saint Elizabeth, you are the Patron Saint for young brides. Please convince Eden that she's not a bridezilla and that she can do this. Also convince the Pope to name a Patron Saint for junior bridesmaids, because I could really use some help.* "You can do it. I know you can. You got through high school. You have a job, and you go to school, and you're moving to Illinois. You can do anything, Eden."

"I'm skipping dinner. Tell them I'm sick."

I put the skirt and tank top on the bed next to her. "You can't leave Justin hanging like that. If Justin can do this, then you can do this. You're a team, right?"

With her eyes closed, Eden takes a few deep breaths. She inhales through her nose and blows the air through her lips. Finally she opens her eyes. "I learned that in our support group. It helps." She stands up and holds the clothes against her body. "Do you really think it looks nice? Or is it just because it's the only skirt in my closet?"

"I really love this skirt. Really."

"Because I also have some skorts."

I try to sound like Paula T, Wedding Consultant. "You are not wearing a skort to a wedding dinner."

"Okay. Thanks, Mary. I like this skirt." I'm proud I actually did something to help the bride. Then Eden frowns and points out the window. "Unbelievable! Grandma's driving away. She left without us."

I shake my head. "Grandzilla." Eden actually throws her head back and laughs.

Grandma gives us a cold smile when we arrive at the restaurant twenty minutes late. Eden whispers to her for a minute; then they hug. Grandma can't stay mad at Eden.

Right away I can tell Justin's parents are serious types. Their smiles seem forced, and they're dressed like we're all attending a business dinner. It's ninety degrees outside, and his mom is wearing a black blazer. Their names: Jason and Jolene Jackson. Justin's brother Joshua is the best man, but he couldn't make it to dinner. Jason, Jolene, Justin, and Joshua Jackson. It's kind of ridiculous, but I shouldn't judge a family of "J" people since mine is over-populated with Marys. There's me, Mary Margaret. Then Eden Mary, Aunt Margaret "Maggie" Mary, Mom Bernice "Bernie" Mary, and Grandma Mary Nadine. Nope. No judgment from me.

I wonder if Nick's family does Vietnamese stuff like

Grandma with her German meals and Uncle Will with his Irish soda bread. What do they serve in Vietnamese restaurants? Is it like Chinese food? My family thinks the fried rice from the food court is too spicy. I'm lost in thoughts about Nick when Luke kicks my leg. He's balancing his spoon on his nose. I whisper, "Stop it. They'll think we're hillbillies."

"What are hillbillies?" He lets the spoon drop on his lap.

"People who put spoons on their noses at nice restaurants."

The adults don't notice. They're gabbing about gas prices. Grandma's laptop sits at the corner of the table. My parents' faces are trapped in the screen, looking bored, but they smile and lean forward, trying to hear the conversation.

"Mary?" Grandma asks.

"Yes?"

"Justin's mother asked about your dress."

"Oh." I need to pay attention. Bridesmaids can't zone out of the conversation just because it's boring. "It's pink. There's a ribbon in back, and the skirt has lace and beads and is quite large." I look at Eden, who's staring at her napkin. "And it's very beautiful. Extremely beautiful."

"Sounds lovely," Mrs. Jackson says. "Tell me about the wedding dress, Eden."

Eden breathes in through her nose and out her mouth before answering. "It's white. The color is white or the candlelight shade of white. It's a pretty white dress."

"It's simple but elegant," Grandma says. "Classic. You know how you see wedding dresses in pictures from twenty years ago and chuckle because they're so tacky? This is a dress that will stand the test of time."

Aunt Maggie says, "I still love my dress. Doesn't matter what anyone says."

"I wasn't able to do much for my daughters when they got married." Grandma's smile fades and her voice turns coarse. "My husband was disabled, and both girls got engaged at the same time. We had a double wedding to cut expenses. My friends from church made soup and ham sandwiches for the reception and also helped me make bouquets and centerpieces with fake flowers. Those were tough times."

"Mother, we wouldn't change a thing about our wedding. Isn't that right, Will?"

Uncle Will snaps to attention. "Right. Gas prices. Definitely too high."

Grandma shakes her head. "For goodness sake! We're

done talking about gas. Anyway, the only thing that matters is we have a spectacular wedding for a spectacular couple. Am I right?"

The Jacksons sip water while Aunt Maggie elbows Uncle Will and whispers, "Pay attention!" He's going to say something, and it's probably going to be embarrassing, so I jump into the conversation. "You're right. Uncle Will is right about gas prices, and you're right about the spectacularness of the wedding." I'm not even sure "spectacularness" is a word, but it makes Grandma smile.

Two waiters enter with trays and put salads in front of everyone. Uncle Will frowns. "Is this one of those places where the food comes in shifts?"

Aunt Maggie whispers to him. "Yes. We preordered dinner."

Uncle Will is not capable of whispering. He says, "It's too complicated. When are we supposed to pray? Before the salad? After the soup?"

"You can say a silent prayer right now. Silent," Grandma says.

"Keep my salad." Uncle Will tells the waiter. "I don't eat leaves. And you can bring me two beers."

"Will!" Aunt Maggie gasps.

"Make it three," Uncle Will says. "Save yourself two trips."

Luke hands his salad back to the waiter. "I don't eat leaves, either."

"Luke!" I gasp just like Aunt Maggie.

I expect Grandma to make Luke taste the salad, but she's not interested in the food. She clears her throat. "Let's talk about the music."

Justin and Eden glance at each other.

Mrs. Jackson sits up straight. "Justin had mentioned having a harpist during the dinner and leaving it at that. It would be lovely background music. My niece plays harp, and she says she'll do it for free as her gift to Eden and Justin."

"Perfect!" Grandma said. "Dinner music will be a nice touch. But I'm talking about the reception. A wedding without a dance is like half a wedding."

"I'm not much of a dancer," Justin stammers. "Two left feet. That's me."

"The people in our family aren't dancers," Mrs. Jackson says.

I know Eden doesn't want a dance, but I also know Grandma *does*. So what do I say?

"Every dance has dancers and watchers." Grandma chuckles. "The Collins family will be the dancers and the Jacksons can be the watchers. After a few beers, Justin will be doing the Chicken Dance with everyone else."

Luke stands to demonstrate the Chicken Dance. He flaps his arms like a bird, squats, jumps up, and claps, humming the tune as he moves. Everyone laughs. My parents aren't laughing, though. Mom's eyes are closed, and Dad's hand is frozen mid air, like he was going to itch his nose right when the Internet connection broke.

After Luke takes his bow, Mr. Jackson says, "We don't drink very often. Justin thought the wedding could be alcohol free."

Uncle Will snorts. "You people can drink apple juice. My family will be drinking beer."

"I'm sorry," Mrs. Jackson says. "Justin told us you're very devout in your...church...so I guess we assumed you didn't drink or dance."

Grandma and Uncle Will laugh. Aunt Maggie says, "Jesus turned water into wine at weddings. That's the only endorsement we need."

"Jesus approves of polka," Grandma says. "I guarantee it."

I feel sorry for Eden. Her face is the color of the tomato soup the waiters just delivered. Aunt Maggie says, "It's going to be tricky finding a band on such short notice. We're lucky we were able to find a church and a reception hall."

Here's my chance. "Since you probably can't find a band, maybe we should give up that idea and just focus on the ceremony and the food and the cake. How does that sound?"

I turn to Eden so she can at least nod her agreement, but Grandma is already talking. "We'll get a band. I'll figure it out. Also, I think we should have an ice sculpture. I found a company that can do a sculpture of the heads of the bride and groom!"

"Cool!" Luke says.

"Grandma, how about—"

She interrupts me and continues, "Fancy cupcakes are so popular these days. I thought we could get a small wedding cake and then a variety of cupcakes. We could order little plastic coins with the words *Eden and Justin* and press the coins into the frosting and then everyone would have a little keepsake from the wedding." She turns to Eden. "What do you think, Eden?"

Before Eden can blush, Aunt Maggie has something to say. "I asked the people at the reception hall if we can have a big screen in the corner so we can put together a slide show of photos."

I say, "Aunt Maggie, maybe we could—"

Again, Grandma shuts me down. She lists the kinds of photos she wants in the slideshow—baptism, birthday parties, Christmas—and I notice Luke is trying to do the Chicken Dance with a spoon on his nose. I grab his arm and pull him back into his chair. "Stop!"

"I'm bored," he whispers.

"If you don't knock if off, I'm going to send a prayer to the Pope right now!"

He presses his lips into a full pout, but he stays in his chair. Now it's time to tackle Grandma. I squeeze my napkin and say, "You know, possibly a wedding shouldn't have a dance if the bride and groom aren't dancers."

Uncle Will says, "The wedding is for the couple, but the reception is for family. We have three hundred relatives coming to this, plus whoever you people are inviting. What are they supposed to do? Knit and sip apple juice? There will be a dance, there will be a band, there will be beer."

"Oh my," Mrs. Jackson says, "such a large wedding. Your church must be the size of an amphitheater."

"There's no such thing as a small Catholic church,"

Grandma says. "And there's no such thing as a small Catholic wedding. Is there, Eden?"

Eden is saved by the servers, who bring in trays with plates of lasagna. They clear the soup bowls and serve our dinner. Under his breath Uncle Will says, "Bless UsLordAndTheseGiftsAmen." Aunt Maggie whispers something to him. He holds out his glass of beer, clears his throat, and says, "A toast to the bride and groom."

We clink glasses and say, "Cheers!"

Chapter Sixteen

There's going to be a wedding
in 26 days

GRANDMA HAS COOKED A HUGE BREAKFAST: EGGS, sausage, fried potatoes, fruit, and homemade kolaches, a German sweet bun. Mom and Dad are here for Eden's shower, and having all of us in the same house feels like Christmas. I can't stay mad at Mom even though it's her fault the body of Christ is in my rosary box. The second we hugged and I smelled her—that mix of hairspray and mint gum—I felt like crying. I've been missing her. Instantly I decided I wouldn't tell her about the Communion wafer. After months of stress and sadness, she finally looks relaxed and happy. I don't want the stress and sadness to come back. I'll think of something.

I miss Dad, too, but it's harder with Mom. When I think about her, I get needles in my stomach. Award-winning nice girls don't stay mad at their moms. They fill up their moms' Patron Saint pages with prayer stars. I promise to pray for her three or four times a day, whatever it takes to catch up to the number of stars on Dad's page.

Luke is too excited to eat. He's constantly interrupting with random things. I'm glad Eden's at work because all his yammering might be stressful. Uncle Will tells Dad about the gas prices on the west coast, and Luke says, "Grandma and me went to the waterpark and we went down the tallest slide on this raft and Grandma screamed 'help me Lord' the whole time."

"Luke, have some manners," Mom says. "Uncle Will was talking."

Uncle Will laughs. "Let the kid talk to his dad."

"And we're going to a museum next week and I think it will be boring but Grandma says it will be good for my mind," Luke says. Every day, Grandma has an agenda for us that includes parks or the library or a swimming pool. She even plays soccer with Luke in the backyard. He's in the best summer camp of his life.

"It will be good for your mind." Dad rumples Luke's

hair. "And Mary, what's been the highlight of your summer so far?"

"Eden and I are working on a massive puzzle."

Luke nearly shouts, "Mary spends all her time in Nick's driveway!"

"Who's Nick?" Mom asks.

"The neighbor boy," Luke says. "He's from China."

"He's Vietnamese, Luke. And it's not a big deal."

Mom and Dad swap looks. Dad says, "I'm glad you have a friend here, but I don't want you unsupervised in either house."

I feel my face heating up and want to melt into a puddle underneath the table, but Grandma barks, "Of course she's not unsupervised inside his house. Or this house! What kind of grandmother do you think I am?"

"Why?" Luke asks. "Do you think they'll kiss?"

"Luke!" I kick him under the table.

"That's enough." Grandma's voice makes Luke shut his mouth and sit still. I give a silent thanks to Saint Ann, Patron Saint of grandmothers. Grandma says, "Let's change the subject. Have you found a house?"

"It's crazy," Mom says. "The oil boom has brought in so many people that housing is scarce, but we have a lead on a house we can rent. How about Eden and Justin? Have they found a place in Illinois?"

Without a pause, Grandma bursts into tears. I'm stunned. I've never seen Grandma cry. Luke and Dad stop chewing and stare. Mom rubs her shoulder. "I'm sorry," Grandma says. "I'm happy for Eden. Really. It's just... I'll miss her. That's all."

"I can hardly stand it myself." Aunt Maggie wipes her eyes with a napkin.

Luke hugs Grandma. "We can visit Eden on the computer."

"And it gives us a reason to go to Chicago," I say. "I'd love to go there."

"Of course." Grandma sniffles. "But ever since my husband died, God bless his soul, it's been Eden and me going to Friday night bingo and Tuesday bargain movie night. We shop together and have lunch. She's my best friend. Is that ridiculous?"

Maybe it's not ridiculous, but it's *weird*. Still, we shake our heads no. Poor Grandma. She's spent all her time being Eden's friend instead of being with people her own age. Now Eden has Justin, and Grandma's got nothing to do on Friday nights except argue with Uncle Will about German beer. Sometimes it's hard to feel sorry for Grandma. This isn't one of those times.

Officially, I'm hosting the shower since I'm the junior bridesmaid. That's what the invitation said, but Grandma planned everything. My only assignment is decorating. While Grandma, Mom, and Aunt Maggie prepare food and clean, Luke and I tie balloons to a chair Dad moved to the front window where Eden will sit like some sort of bride queen. I'll be in a folding chair next to her writing down who gave her which presents.

Grandma hands crepe paper to Luke and me. "String this up so it looks nice. Hurry because your dad and Uncle Will are ready to take you fishing."

No boys allowed at this shower.

At two o'clock, the guests began to arrive: Eden's friend Emma from the hospital laundry; Mom and Aunt Maggie's cousins, Kate, Bridget, Mary Ellen, and Mary Alice (more Marys!); and Grandma's church friends Elaine, Connie, and Beth; and a coworker of Aunt Maggie's named Tracy.

Eden perches in her special chair, the balloons floating above her head like pastel clouds. Immediately Grandma announces the games, which is probably supposed to be my job. I'm happy sitting quietly next to Eden. Then Grandma calls on me.

"Mary, I need you to be my assistant." She hands me a bowl filled with uncooked rice and tiny safety pins. Then she gives me a blindfold. "We each get one minute to find as many safety pins as possible."

Cousin Bridget claps. "I love this game! You can barely feel the difference between the safety pins and the rice."

I tie the blindfold around her eyes, swish the bowl to make sure everything is mixed up, and put it on her lap.

Apparently the game loves her, too, because nobody pulls out more pins. Even with a Band-Aid on her finger, she finds twelve pins. Mary Alice (or is it Mary Ellen?) finds only one. I get five, but I don't try very hard. It seems tacky for the junior bridesmaid to win. For her prize, Bridget gets a big candle scented like pumpkin spice. Everyone gushes over the smell, and Mom says, "Wish I'd won this." Mom doesn't even like the smell of pumpkin pie. Does she ever say anything and mean it?

For the next game, Grandma brings out eight plastic baggies filled with spices and a notebook. "Time to spice up this party!" She says with an exaggerated wink. Each guest puts on the blindfold while Grandma holds each spice bag in front of them. They sniff and guess what the spice might be, and I keep track of their answers in the notebook. Before the bags go to the next person, Grandma mixes up the order.

When it's Mom's turn, she inhales and says, "I guess I need time to think about this," and everyone laughs.

I lean to Eden and whisper, "What's so funny?"

"She means t-h-y-m-e as in the spice. It's a pun."

"Oh."

"Hurry up already," Aunt Maggie says.

"I'm comin'," Mom says, and the ladies roar with laughter.

Eden whispers to me again. "Another spice joke. She's coming. *Cumin*, coming."

"Oh." My smile hides frustration. I don't think she's funny. The feeling of missing her is blending into the feeling of being mad at her. Instead of making jokes, instead of having long talks with Aunt Maggie about the wedding and North Dakota, she should ask me how it's going. All she wants to hear is we're happy, happy, happy—not that Uncle Will got sick and Luke spit a Communion wafer on my dress and now it's a dried-up glob in my rosary box.

When the spice game finally ends, I tally the points. Emma gets the prize, a set of brass candle stick holders.

"For our last activity, everyone needs a pen." Grandma says.

She hands out index cards and tells everyone to write words of wisdom about marriage for the bride. When Eden opens a gift, I'm supposed to read that woman's advice. At least Grandma is smart enough not to make Eden read them. Eden would dash out of the house and never come back, and I mean *never.*

Just then the lawn mower rumbles. From the window I see Nick starting to cut the first strip by the curb. A frown splits Grandma's face. "Mary, will you go outside and tell him mowing will have to wait?"

I dart outside, catch up to Nick, and tap him on the shoulder. He grins when he sees me. The mower stops.

I say, "We're having a wedding shower for Eden, so my grandma wants to know if you'll mow after everyone leaves."

"Okay. A shower, huh? Are you having fun?"

"It's like a first-grade birthday party. We're playing games and winning prizes."

"What kind of games?"

"Like games involving spices. I had no idea my mom's sense of humor is so bad. She's making spice jokes."

"Can't wait to hear about it. You want to shoot buckets later?"

"My parents are leaving tomorrow. We're having a family dinner tonight."

"So tomorrow?"

"Sure."

"Mary!" Grandma shouts from the window. "That's enough."

Quietly I say, "I can't dilly dally."

"Get moving, you rapscallion," Nick whispers. We crack up. Nick pushes the lawn mower back to Uncle Will's garage, and I go back to the shower. There are a stack of index cards waiting on my chair for me to read. I settle in next to Eden and read the first card.

"This is from Elaine. 'Love is patient and kind.'" Such a cheat. That's straight from the Bible. Eden opens the present and pulls out a stack of kitchen towels, each embroidered with a day of the week. That morning, I'd looked for a Patron Saint of bridal showers and couldn't find one, but there is a Patron Saint of returning unwanted gifts, Saint Emma.

"Thank you so, so very much." Eden is starting to

sweat. She even smells sweaty, and her breath isn't a garden of roses, either.

Her anxiety is making *me* nervous. I clear my throat and say, "The next card is from Tracy. It says, 'Never go to bed angry with each other. Always apologize.'"

Eden nods and finds a hand mixer in the next box. While she passes the gift around, Grandma brings us glasses of punch. She squeezes my shoulder and says, "You're doing great. Are you having fun?"

"Of course!"

Truthfully, it's the longest afternoon of my life. All I want to do is play basketball with the rapscallion next door.

There's going to be a wedding in **23** days

"Mary Margaret Miller! Are you in a coma? It's nearly eleven!"

My eyes peel open. Grandma's hovering over me. "Up and at 'em! We've got a great day planned. There's a park outside the city with a lake and a beach. I packed a picnic. Get your swimsuit on, and let's hit the road."

I groan. I don't want to go to the beach with Luke. I want to shoot baskets with Nick.

"Sleeping Beauty, you're wasting a beautiful, sunny day."

"I think I slept so late because I have a headache. Maybe I'll just stay here."

"I have aspirin," Grandma says. "You'll be cured by the time we get there. We'll meet you outside."

"I'm still really tired."

Grandma threads her fingers with mine and squeezes my hand. "Honey, I know its tough for you and Luke because your parents left. The best thing is to get out of the house and do something special. No moping."

I know it's not worth wasting any more words, so I get out of bed.

"Good girl," Grandma says. "We'll see you outside in a few minutes."

I change into my suit and a cover up. Downstairs I dig through boxes of cereal, but I don't find anything I like. I spot the leftover cake from the shower. We ate the "Congratu" part of the "Congratulations." Nobody will notice the missing "la," so I make that breakfast. I rinse it down with a glass of milk and head outside where Grandma and Luke are talking to Nick. I freeze. Grandma waves me over, but I want to run back into the house. There is only a 1 percent chance this isn't going to be humiliating.

She says, "I was just telling Nick he must come with us. It's good for you to be with someone your own age."

"Oh." I avoid Nick's eyes and hope Luke doesn't say something stupid.

"I don't think my mom will let me," Nick says.

Grandma asks, "Is she home? Or at work?"

"She's on her summer schedule, so she's home now. But she'll say no."

"Well, then, I'll just have a chat with her."

Grandma knocks on the door. I shrug, like *What can you do?* and he half smiles. His mom opens the door and listens to Grandma. I think she's saying no, but mostly there's the melody of Grandma's words. Finally Grandma calls to us. "Go get changed, Nick. Mary, go back inside and pack some snacks. I have drinks in a cooler, but we should have food, too. Let's hit the road!"

Nick looks shocked, almost dazed. He says, "I can't believe she said yes."

I say, "My grandmother is very persuasive." It'll be fun to be with Nick at the beach, but I'm worried Grandma will embarrass me. She can't help herself. And what if Luke makes kissing noises or asks Nick about being Chinese? I want to hang out with Nick, but not with Nick *and* my family.

Inside the house I pack chips and granola bars in a paper bag. The chocolate chip cookies will melt, so I leave them in the cupboard. I'm wondering if I should make sandwiches when I hear Nick's voice. "Your grandma says to not make sandwiches because she'll buy hotdogs."

"Oh." I'm hit by nerves all over again, and I say a quick prayer. *Dear Holy Saint John Bosco, Patron Saint of boys, please make sure Nick is in the bathroom if Grandma and Luke say something ridiculous.* "I guess I've got everything."

"Let's go." Nick grabs the bag, and we head to the door. But then Nick stops. His head shifts as he studies the pictures on each side of the front door. There's one of Jesus on the right and one of Mary on the left. Those pictures have been there for as long as I can remember. We have a set in Holmestrand, too. He shakes his head. "That's crazy!"

"What?"

"Those Jesus and Mary pictures. They're blond!"

"So?"

"So they weren't blond," he says.

I don't know where he's going with this. I say, "You don't know that."

"People in Jerusalem aren't blond. Jesus and Mary looked like Arabs. Or they could've been black. The region is very close to Africa."

"Jesus was from the Jewish race. I know that."

"Jew doesn't mean race," he says. "It's not a race. It's a religion. We talked about it in my church."

"What church?"

"Unitarian. You know how most kids have church programs where they memorize bible verses? In my church we study world religions. It's a very intellectual church."

I cross my arms. "Are you saying my church is not intellectual?"

He raises his eyebrows. "All churches are based on faith to some degree. It's just Catholics seem to have a lot of…there's some hocus-pocus in your tradition."

Nick doesn't look cute anymore. He looks like the biggest jerk ever. "Excuse me? I didn't realize you were an expert on the Middle East *and* Catholics."

"It'd take a miracle to make these pictures historically accurate. That's all I'm saying."

I open the door and stomp to the car.

All the way to the beach I'm silently fuming about Nick and his intellectual church. Even if he's right about blond Mary and Jesus—and maybe he has a point—he's wrong about Catholics and hocus-pocus. Sure, we do some weird things, like having priests chant over Communion wafers and turn them into the actual body of Jesus. Our priests wear goofy robes, we do the sit-kneel-stand thing, and we have a saint for carnival workers. But we're not practicing voodoo. We're Christians.

Nick's not quiet, though. He's talking to Grandma and Luke talk about the Star Wars series, which they just binge watched. Grandma says, "I just could not believe Darth Vader was Luke's father!"

This makes Nick laugh really hard. Luke announces, "Now we all have to name our favorite Star Wars characters."

"Yoda," Grandma says. "I like wise, old people."

"Han Solo," Nick says.

"I like Anakin when he was a kid before he turns to the dark side and tries to rule the galaxy," Luke says. "What about you, Mary?"

"I don't have an opinion."

"I also like Leia," Grandma says. "I like her hairstyles."

That makes Nick and Luke completely crack up. Luke says, "Eden should get that cinnamon-roll hairstyle for her wedding."

I have a moment of panic because, seriously, Grandma is the kind of person who would bring Star Wars pictures to the hairstylist and insist that's how Eden should look.

But she laughs, and I'm relieved she knows it's a joke. All the laughter makes it hard to stay angry. It's pretty cool Nick can talk and joke with Grandma and Luke like he's known them forever. If I was in a car with Nick's family, my lips would freeze shut.

Nick says, "Princess Leia does wear a lot of white." He smiles at me, and the last bits of my anger fade.

"Leia was my favorite character," I say. "But now it's Rey."

"Mary?" Luke pokes the back of my head. "Will you play Marco Polo? I want to find you!"

"You can't play Marco Polo at a crowded beach. You end up groping strangers."

"If it's not crowded will you play? Please?"

I sigh. "Okay." I know this means I'll end up playing—crowds or no crowds. Luke is as persistent as Grandma.

As soon as we're parked and unpacked, Grandma and Luke rush to the water while Nick and I sit on the beach towels. I call to Grandma, "I'll watch our stuff for a while."

I feel weird in my swimming suit, which suddenly seems too small, even though it's a one-piece. But Nick's not looking at me. He's scanning the beach.

"I've never been to this beach," he says. "I'm more of a pool guy."

"Me, too."

He pushes sand around with his feet like they're snow-plows. "Look, I'm sorry I was a jerk about your Caucasian Mary and Jesus. My parents are professors. I've been raised by people with strong opinions who like to argue."

"Oh."

"And now that they're divorced, they really, really like to argue. You probably don't understand because Catholics aren't supposed to get divorced. It's a big sin, right?"

"Catholics get divorced. They're not supposed to, but they do. The Pope doesn't sentence us to some big Catholic jail for breaking rules."

"I should just shut up," Nick says. "Is there a Patron Saint for people with big mouths?"

"Yes. Saint Nicholas."

"Are you serious?"

I laugh. "No, I'm kidding."

"You totally had me."

Grandma calls from the water, "Use the sunscreen!" I look around for the bottle, but this isn't fast enough for Grandma, who shouts, "Do it now! You'll thank me when you're fifty and your skin is smooth and cancer-free!"

I pull the sunscreen from the bag, squirt some on my legs, arms, and face. As I rub it in, Nick takes the bottle and smears the lotion on himself. He says, "I'm a big mouth, but even big mouths have friends. I know you haven't seen anyone at my house all summer, but it's not because I'm a jerk. I'm grounded until the end of July."

"Oh."

I've never been grounded. Other than Brent Helzinski, I've never been in trouble. Even after Mom got the phone call from the principal about Brent, she didn't ground me. She sent me to Confession and gave me a short lecture about Jesus not fighting the bullies who were going to crucify him. I wanted to say Jesus had orders directly from God, but I knew that was not a winning strategy.

Nick asks, "You want to know why I'm grounded?"

"Do you want to tell me?"

"Yes and no. I mean you're so churchy, what if you don't like me anymore?"

"I punched a guy by my locker and got detention. Is it worse than that?" The words left my mouth before I had time to think about them. But I'm not flooded with embarrassment. I'm kind of relieved, which is weird. Nick is probably the only person I know who won't judge me.

He blinks like there's sand in his eyes. "Seriously? You've got to tell me that story."

"You go first."

"Okay. I'm grounded because I shoplifted. And it wasn't the first time, and it wasn't the first time I got caught."

We had shoplifters in the store but not very often. People don't tend to steal nails and extension cords. But before we closed for good, a lady tried to steal a flashlight that was already half price because of the going-out-of-business sale. Stealing is a sin no matter what the price. Why would Nick do something like that? He seems so nice.

"What'd you take?"

"The first couple times? Candy, mostly. Then I graduated to bigger things. Once I took a gallon of milk from the gas station, and nobody even noticed. I'd gone to the store on the way home from school, and I slipped the milk into my backpack. And I mean, why milk? How stupid is that? My mom buys groceries. It's not like I'm from a milk-free home."

"Then why? I don't get it."

"I just get mad. It's like these big stores rule the planet or something. Their stupid ads tell us what to buy, their prices tell us how much to spend, they pollute the world with their plastic junk and plastic bags. Chains control the world. These stores have bigger bank accounts than the economy of Ecuador. Did you know that?"

I didn't know companies made more money than countries, but I'm not surprised. Home Supply Station probably *owns* Ecuador. I felt relieved when I realized Nick wouldn't judge me, so I'm not going to judge him, either. "I hate chains, too. Home Supply Station ruined my family's business. I hate Home Supply Station so much I don't care if people steal from them."

"Well, I won't," Nick says. "I'm done stealing. The funny thing is my mom completely agrees with me, except for the stealing, of course. She freaked out when I got caught. So we've been talking about stuff I can do to fight it that's not illegal. My church youth group might start a campaign to get people to shop local."

"Sign me up!" Suddenly Nick's church sounds cool. "I've never heard of a church doing something like that. My church youth group does things like rake leaves for old people. What you're doing sounds like politics."

"My parents say everything is politics."

"Hey, if you're grounded, how come you're here?"

"Your grandma wouldn't take no for an answer." Nick grins. "Now it's your turn. Who did you hit and why?"

I'm ready to tell the story—the whole story, for the first time. But Luke sloshes out of the water and stands over us. "Aren't you coming in?"

"In a few minutes," I say.

Grandma yells, "Mary Margaret Miller! We're at the beach to enjoy the water. Get in here!"

Even Nick knows there's no point in arguing. He stands and brushes the sand off his legs. "Later, I guess."

"Marco Polo!" Luke shouts. "I'll go first."

ABOUT BRENT HELZINSKI AND ME

Brent and his buddies Eric and Jude came to the Halloween party as a biker gang. Brent's stomach pudged out from a leather vest. A chain dangled from the pockets of black jeans. On his arm was a fake tattoo of a snake. It curled from his wrist to the seam of his T-shirt.

Chapter Eighteen

There's going to be a wedding in 16 days

BLESSED IMELDA IS OBVIOUSLY DEALING WITH A LOT OF Communion problems. It's like I called her on the phone, and she put me on hold.

I decide to look online for an answer. I search the phrase "proper disposal of Communion wafer" and find lots of information from non-Catholic churches like Lutheran and Presbyterian. One church pastor reports that he feeds unused wafers to the birds. *To the birds!* Another site says it doesn't matter what you do with the wafers because Communion is symbolic and considering it the literal body of Christ is superstitious. *Superstitious?* Do other churches think Catholics are full of hocus-pocus?

I feel guilty just reading that stuff, so I do a quick sign of the cross and add the word "Catholic" to my search. I find a question-and-answer site with a priest. A man asks what's supposed to happen if a parishioner drops the wafer on the floor. The priest says he should scoop it up as fast as possible and pop it in his mouth, because Communion isn't symbolic. It's sacred.

None of this helps. It's time to call Mom and get her to fix it. The latest report is my parents found a house to rent, and Mom has job interviews lined up. She's not working double shifts at the gas station and missing Dad. The dark circles under her eyes are probably gone. She can handle it.

Before I find my phone, Eden bursts into the room, flops on the bed, and puts the pillow over her face.

"What's wrong?"

The pillow swallows her mumbling, so I pull it away from her and sit on the bed. "Eden?"

"Our family is crazy. Not good crazy, either. Bad crazy." She sits up. "There's a dress war."

"But we have dresses."

"Not us. Them. Grandma says she and Mom and Aunt Bernie have to wear pink because you're wearing pink. Mom and Aunt Bernie say pink isn't good for older people, plus your mom already bought a blue dress. Grandma's mad because your mom didn't consult with anyone on the dress, and now she's ruining the wedding pictures. Your mom cut the tags off the dress, and the store won't take it back, and your dad doesn't want her to spend money on a different dress. Grandma's mad at both your parents. My mom is completely stressed out. She's not sure if she should wear pink and match Grandma, or blue and match your mom, and basically none of them are speaking."

Another family conflict and another money problem. I picture the dark circles returning to Mom's eyes. I say a quick prayer. *Dear Holy Blessed Imelda, I'm back.*

Eden bolts out of bed and pulls the table with the puzzle between our beds. "We have to finish this before the wedding. It's important."

"It took thousands of years to make the Grand Canyon. We need more than one summer to finish."

"We need to. We have to." Eden sounds frantic.

"I don't get it."

"All I know is when I'm doing this puzzle, I'm not thinking about anything else."

She's deep in concentration within minutes. I want to ask her about blond Jesus and blond Mary, but she seems to be relaxing. Plus, I know Nick is right. Unless Jesus and Mary walked from Sweden to Jerusalem, their skin is darker. I think it's a marketing thing. People want Jesus to look like them or, I guess, they want to look like Jesus. For hundreds of years, Popes gave Caucasian Catholics a Caucasian Jesus. If I went to a Catholic Church in Africa, I probably wouldn't find pictures of Caucasian Jesus and Mary. Obviously the Pope thought, *Hey, if we want to grow the membership in Africa, we need to make an African Jesus and Mary.*

I'm tired of thinking about all of it—church pictures, the Communion wafer, sin, and prayer. Mostly I'm tired of sending out prayers to the Patron Saints and getting silence in return. Blessed Imelda has not solved my wafer problem. Don't even get me started on Saint Sebastian and hardware stores.

Finally Eden looks up. "I do have good news. The first is a surprise, and I have to tell someone or I'll explode." I've never seen Eden look so excited.

"Okay."

She leans forward. "Justin and I agreed we can't afford a honeymoon, but I've been secretly looking for the cheapest possible trip, and I found this incredible deal to go to Las Vegas. We're not the kind of people who go to

Las Vegas, but I found a package with a beautiful hotel, and it includes two shows and a trip to Hoover Dam. So I booked it and paid for it, and Justin doesn't know. So don't breathe a word, okay?"

"Very cool. My lips are sealed," I say. "What's the other news item?"

"Your parents want you and me to make a road trip to your house. We're supposed to make sure the house is in good shape and bring back your dad's suit for the wedding."

"That's awesome!" I think about all the stuff we could do in Holmestrand: see Jessica, eat at Dave's Diner, drive by the lake.

From downstairs comes Grandma's hurry-up-and-I-mean-it voice. "Girls!"

I groan. "Now what?"

Eden hunches over the puzzle. "She bought small cakes from the bakery for us to sample so we can pick a flavor for the wedding."

"I thought we were having cupcakes."

"She found a bakery that will make a wedding cake with a fountain in the middle, and that seems spectacular to her." Her voice is flat. "All we have to do is pick a flavor."

"A fountain? You're kidding."

"I'm not known for being a kidder."

Grandma yells again. I get as far as the bathroom when I notice Eden isn't with me. I pop my head back into her room. "Aren't you coming?"

"Please tell her my stomach hurts. Besides, I won't be eating cake at the wedding."

"What do you mean?"

"Please, Mary. Just go downstairs before she goes crazy. You can decide. I don't care."

Downstairs Nick is sitting at the table next to Luke and Uncle Will. I quickly smooth my hair and straighten my shirt. "I invited our neighbor to the tasting." Grandma winks, and I want to disappear—or make Grandma disappear—but Nick doesn't notice. He's smelling the cake Luke has perched under his nose.

"Lemon?" Luke asks.

"I definitely smell lemon."

Luke makes a face. "I don't like fruit or vegetables in my cake."

"If lemons were important, they'd grow them in Ireland," Uncle Will says.

Grandma slaps the table. "Please! I need all of you to have an open mind. There are five samples. We have white cake with raspberry filling, lemon cake, carrot cake, red velvet cake, and plain white cake. Drink milk in between bites so you're getting an honest and true taste." She looks at me. "Where's Eden?"

"She says her stomach hurts, and we should pick." Here I am truth-stretching to Grandma, just like Mom.

"I suppose her anxiety is kicking in." Grandma sighs. "Why don't you and Nick take your samples to the porch and eat out there? I have a feeling we'll be battling over the lemon and raspberries and carrots in here. I don't want you and Nick influenced by these two." She points at Luke and Uncle Will.

My mood instantly improves. I get to hang out with Nick and escape Grandma and Uncle Will's bickering. Nick and I take our plates to the porch and sit on the wicker bench. I can hear Uncle Will complaining about the carrot cake through the door. Nick stabs his fork in the cake and eats.

"Your uncle is so wrong. This carrot cake is epic." He licks a dab of frosting off his thumb. "I'd mow the lawn for free all summer for one piece of this cake." He takes a bite of the lemon cake, and closes his eyes. "Oh my God. I just changed my mind. Why isn't all cake made with lemon? There should be a law. How come you're not eating? This is amazing."

"I'm with Luke on this one. Cake shouldn't be contaminated with vegetables or fruit."

"You have to try it. We're under orders. Don't dilly dally."

I laugh and take a bite of the lemon cake. "Yuck. It reminds me of furniture polish."

"I'll take the rest of it."

While he eats his cake samples and mine, too, I start talking about the wedding story, and once I start, it all comes tumbling out. I tell him about shopping for the dresses, Eden's shower, and the dinner with Justin's parents. "This cake we're sampling? Grandma is ordering it with a fountain in the middle. Eden doesn't want that. And I should be able to stand up and say no, and I try, but it's not working."

"It's her wedding. It's not your job."

"Eden has a real condition, so it actually is my job. A bridesmaid is supposed to help deal with the stress and conflict involved in a wedding. And it's not easy. My family is making me crazy. I'd like to . . . I don't know . . ."

Nick raises his eyebrows. "Punch someone?"

It takes me a few seconds to remember our conversation at the beach. Talking about it seemed like a good idea while we were sitting in the sun, but now I'm not sure. "It's not that interesting."

"Come on. Fair is fair."

"First I should tell you that I won a state award for being this great church youth group member," I say. "That's important because you'll either like the irony, or you'll cut me some slack."

He sets down the plate. If anyone will understand, it's a shoplifting, skateboarding basketball player who thinks Caucasian Jesus is a joke. I take a breath. I'm ready.

I almost didn't go to Ryan Dorman's Halloween party because he'd invited the whole class. That meant Brent Helzinski would be there, and he'd been tormenting me for weeks. I kicked a ball, and it smashed his face, and he was out to get me. But I figured he'd behave himself at a party.

The party was in Ryan's basement, and it was perfect—dark, creepy, damp. Fake tarantulas and bats dangled from the ceiling, and his mom made mummies and ghosts and propped them by a big table with candy, chips, cheese, crackers, and a cake decorated like a cemetery. There were games, too. Pin the wart on the witch, a zombie dance-off, speed-mummy-wrapping, and bobbing for apples.

I was dressed as Dorothy from The Wizard of Oz, *a costume recycled from last year because Mom didn't want to spend money on something new. Jessica was dressed as Hermione from Harry Potter. We were by the apple-bobbing station talking to Ryan and Josh Bloomquist. Nobody was bobbing for apples because they didn't want to mess up their costumes. It looked like fun, though.*

Brent waddled over. "Hey Little Bo Peep, you afraid to get wet?"

He was dressed as a motorcycle guy with tight pants—all his pants were tight—and a leather vest. He had a mullet wig and a fake tattoo of a snake slithering up his arm. Ryan and Josh were both dressed as Superman but neither said a word to Brent. So much for superheroes. But I kind of understood. I'd seen Brent pick on lots of people, and I'd done the same thing as Ryan and Josh—suddenly act distracted or like I couldn't hear or see what was happening.

Brent pulled on my pigtail and laughed. Only an idiot can't tell the difference between Dorothy and Little Bo Peep. But I ignored him. That's what you're supposed to do with bullies. Ignore them. Then he pulled my hair again.

I was so irritated. I said, "Knock it off!"

"Let's bob for apples," he said. "If you get more than me, I won't pull your hair for the rest of the night."

"I'm not having a contest with you."

He got closer—too close. I could smell the nacho cheese chips on his breath. He'd been calling me Scary Mary and saying mean things since the ball I kicked nearly broke his nose. Early in the week he pretended to trip in the hallway, which made him "accidentally" push me. Now he was ruining the party. I waited for Josh or Ryan or Jessica to say something. They shifted on their feet and suddenly seemed fascinated by their cups of punch.

"Don't be such a baby," he said, tugging my hair again. His two buddies, Eric Jablonski and Jude Sorenson, were leaning against the wall, laughing. Ryan and Josh wandered away, two cowards in Superman costumes.

Finally Jessica stepped in. "Just take him on, Mary. I don't think Brent can win at anything." She turned to Brent and said, "When she wins, go back to your corner."

"Fine," he said. "I will. The contest will be how many you can get in one minute."

I faced the bin of water. The apples were small, so they looked easy to bite. I leaned over the bin, took a breath, and put my face in the water. It was super cold, but I got an apple immediately.

Suddenly my arms were pulled behind my back and a hand shoved my head to the bottom of the bin. Then someone—Brent, obviously—held my arms and kept my head under water. I tried kicking backward, but mostly I was just thrashing around. I couldn't breathe. I couldn't yell.

Later Jessica told me it was only a few seconds, but in those seconds I thought so many random things. I thought, Am I drowning? My parents will be sad. Will Brent go to Hell? What if there's no Heaven?

And then I was standing up, blinking water, coughing through the apple, which was attached to my teeth. The first thing I heard was Brent laughing and then Jessica yelling, "You're a complete and total pig!" She put her arm around me. Brent went back to his buddies against the wall. Their laughter seemed louder than the music.

Jessica whispered to me. "I'm going to tell Ryan's parents what Brent did."

I shook my head and pulled the apple out of my mouth. My face was wet, so they probably couldn't tell I was crying. Please, please, stop crying, I told myself. The last thing I wanted was Brent seeing me cry.

The tears stopped. Suddenly I felt tall. I felt strong. I was going to get even. It wasn't right to let the bullies run the world. Jesus wants us to turn the other cheek, but even He didn't do it all the time. He got mad—furious, even—at people who did the wrong thing. He stood up to them, and that's what I was going to do. I was going to stand up to Brent.

My little bite made the small apple even smaller, but it was firm enough and big enough to make my point. I wound my arm *back and threw the apple as hard as I could. Brent tried to shift, but he was so slow, he took the apple in the nose. Blood gushed down his face.*

I didn't feel bad. Not for a second. I would've thrown another one except Ryan's parents showed up. Someone had run upstairs to tell them Brent was trying to drown the girl from The Wizard of Oz.

Nick doesn't take a second to think about it. "That guy is a soul-sucking creep. He deserved it. I don't care what the Bible says; I believe in karma. What goes around comes around."

"There's more," I say.

"Right. You said you punched him before spring break. This was a Halloween party. So this thing with King Creep went on all year?"

"Basically. It scared me at first, but I always felt better after I lashed out at Brent. Does that make sense?"

The door opens, and it's Luke. "Grandma says to tell you Nick's mom called and she said he was only supposed to be here thirty minutes and now he's late."

Nick scrapes the last thin line of frosting from his plate with his fork. "I'm going to my dad's for a week. Tell me the rest when I get back, okay?"

"Okay."

Luke pokes Nick's shoulder. "Grandma wants to know what cake you picked."

"Carrot. The lemon is a close second." Nick gives a quick wave as he leaves. "See you later."

The sun is slipping behind the oak trees across the street. I lean back and close my eyes and focus on the birds' song so I don't have to think about Brent and how the story really ended.

"How about you Mary?" Luke asks. "What's your vote?"

"You tell me, buddy. What do you want my vote to be?"

"Plain white cake."

"Then that's my vote."

He runs into the house cheering, "Plain white cake! Plain white cake! Plain white cake!"

There's going to be a wedding
in 15 days

THE DOORBELL RINGS EARLY THE NEXT MORNING. IT'S Nick, standing with his arms behind his back and a grin on his face. "I have something I need to give you."

"Um...do you want to come in?" It seems like a grown-up thing to ask. Eden hasn't left for work yet, so I'm not violating the rule about being unsupervised.

"I can't. My dad's here, so I only have a minute. Last night I was thinking about your big wedding job. I went to the Catholic Church website to find forms to nominate you as Patron Saint for Junior Bridesmaids."

At first I think he's joking. Nick from the intellectual

church, Nick who called Mary "Jesus's baby mama." But his face is serious.

"I don't get it," I say.

"I figured there has to be a sainthood process. That guy didn't randomly become the Patron Saint of carnival workers, right?"

"Right."

"Turns out the process is pretty complicated. You have to go through a Bishop, and the Bishop has to gather evidence, and I guess someone has to prove you made a miracle happen, maybe even two miracles."

"You're such a geek." I'm laughing.

"Obviously," he says.

"You realize I'm the least qualified person in the world, right?" I say it like I'm joking, but it's the truth. Punching boys. Hiding the Body of Christ. Keeping Mom's secret. Nobody's ever going to call me the Blessed Mary Margaret Miller.

"You might be the first kid in a wedding to actually take it seriously. You care. You really want to help Eden. I think you're the real deal."

My face feels warm, so I have to look away.

"Anyway, there was no time for the formal nomination. This is the best I could do." He hands me a button that's a little bigger than a silver dollar. He's covered it with a piece of paper printed with tiny words.

MARY MILLER
PATRON SAINT OF
JUNIOR
BRIDESMAIDS

I squeeze it. I want to hold it against my heart, but I'll do that later, when he's not watching. "This is the greatest button ever made."

"Obviously."

"I mean it. This is the greatest thing ever."

He's quiet, and I'm quiet, and suddenly it's very, very quiet. No cars, no television—just air and happiness.

I can't stop myself. I hug him.

His back stiffens a bit, and he sort of pats my shoulders. I hear Eden thumping down the stairs, so I push him back harder than I mean to.

"Have fun," he says, backing away.

"I'll try."

The door shuts just as Eden comes downstairs wearing her hospital uniform.

"That was Nick. He wanted to tell me he's going to his dad's for a week."

Eden smiles.

"No teasing!" I say.

"I didn't say a word."

"Stop smiling then." I use a stern voice, but I realize I'm grinning, too.

Eden says, "I know you want to see your friend Jessica while we're in Holmestrand, but I can't stay two nights. I got offered an extra shift, and I really need the money. Maybe you can squeeze in a short visit."

"That's okay. I texted Jessica, and she's on vacation with her parents."

"Is there someone else you want to see?"

I think about Jessica, the kids in my youth group, my teammates in soccer. I think about Mr. and Mrs. Swanson, neighbors who always gave Luke and me five dollar bills instead of candy on Halloween, and Joyce the waitress at Dave's Diner who never got our orders straight, Father Benson and his crooked teeth, and even John

Danner and his goofy laugh. When Eden told me about our road trip, I was excited. But now that we're leaving tomorrow, I don't want to go. I've said my goodbyes, and I don't want to say them again.

And worst of all—what if I see Brent Helzinski?

Eden studies me. "Are you okay?"

"Sure. Of course. What about you? Are you okay?"

"I'm fine."

"Good," I say. "We're both fine. Everything's fine."

Later that afternoon, Grandma starts texting me photos. She's with Luke at the flower shop, but I said I needed to stay home and work on the toast I'm supposed to give at the wedding. Because I have no idea what to say.

Even though I escaped the flower shop, she wants my advice. I get photo after photo after photo with Grandma's commentary in all caps.

RED ROSES DON'T GO WITH PINK, RIGHT?

I guess not.

BUT ROSES ARE ELEGANT, RIGHT?

Yes.

Then my phone rings. It's Mom, but there's another text from Grandma, so I let the call roll into voicemail.

PINK CARNATIONS WOULD BE TOO MUCH PINK,
RIGHT?

I know Grandma. The only correct answer is "right."
And I really want to work on the toast I'm supposed to
give, not study photos.

Right.

Less than a minute later I get a text from Mom.

Grandma just texted me flower photos and says
you're at Maggie's. Is it a good time to talk?

Before I can reply, Grandma's back at it.

THIS IS A LILY BUT IT'S TOO WHITE, RIGHT?

Grandma, you have great taste and whatever you
pick will be perfect!!!!

Hopefully all the exclamation points will put a stop to it.
But it doesn't.

I'm typing a note to Mom when I get another message
from Grandma.

DO YOU KNOW WHEN EDEN HAS HER BREAK
TODAY? I WANT TO CALL HER ABOUT THE
OPTIONS.

Then my phone rings, and it's Mom again. So much
for writing a toast. I toss my notebook aside and answer
the phone.

"Hi, Mom."

"How are you sweetie?" She sounds tired. "I figured it'd be easier to call than keep texting."

"I'm good. I'm trying to write the toast I'm supposed to give at the reception. Everything sounds dumb. Will you help me?"

Silence. "Mom?"

"How about when I get there? I need time to think."

"Okay. How'd your job interviews go?"

Silence.

"Mom?"

She sighs. "Nothing has panned out. The towns around here are so small, even smaller than Holmestrand. There's no work. It looks like I'll have to drive nearly an hour to a bigger town."

"That stinks."

"I was at the post office, and I met a man who just moved to the area. We talked about the job market and my retail experience and the hardware store. Turns out he's a manager of a new shopping center about an hour from here. He offered me a job on the spot. He promised he'd let me set my own schedule so I can work while you're in school and be home when you're home."

"Wow!"

"He said I won't have to work weekends."

"That's awesome."

"He said he'll pay me more than starting wages because of my experience."

There's no emotion in her voice. I don't understand. "It sounds perfect, Mom."

"He manages the new Home Supply Station."

I nearly drop the phone. I sit on my bed and wrap the blanket around me. Suddenly I'm cold from head to toe. Neither of us speak. I listen to Mom breathe.

Finally, I croak out words. "What does Dad say?"

"He says maybe this is God's plan."

"God isn't mean and stupid!" I shout.

"Mary, please. I have to take this job, at least until something else comes along."

My stomach boils, and the heat rises to my chest. Even my face burns. "Don't take it. I mean it, Mom. Don't."

"I'm afraid it's the only option right now."

I press the end call button. I hung up on my own mother! I've never done that before. I send a quick, truth-stretching text. Sorry. Lost the connection. Call you later! Xoxo. Then I turn the phone off so I won't hear it ring when she calls back. I need something to throw, but I can't break my phone, and I can't damage Eden's room. I take tissues from the box on Eden's nightstand, wad them into a ball, and throw it as hard as I can. The fistful of tissues floats through the air and lands on the puzzle with the weight of a whisper.

Dear Holy Saint Sebastian, Patron Saint of hardware stores, you're an epic jerk.

Chapter Twenty

There's going to be a wedding in 7 days

THE OUTSIDE OF OUR HOUSE LOOKS PERFECT. THE neighbor who's taking care of the yard is doing fine. Maybe it's because Luke isn't tearing up the grass with his dirt bike and jumping through the sprinkler all summer. The lawn is emerald green, thick, and free of weeds, with yellow flowers planted around the For Sale sign.

Inside, though, there's a layer of dust on everything. While Eden goes out to pick up sub sandwiches—we have strict instructions not to mess up the kitchen—I vacuum and dust. I save my room for last, because it doesn't look like my room anymore, and I hate it. The real estate agent told us to "de-personalize the space," which means strip away the personality. My bed is covered with a new pink bedspread and a bunch of matching pillows with pink and white flowers on them. If I still lived here, those pillows would stay in my closet. Who needs that many pillows? There's nothing on my desk or my dresser. All the pictures, notebooks, and books are in boxes in the basement waiting to be moved to North Dakota.

Eden calls, "I'm back. Let's eat!"

In the kitchen Eden is unloading a grocery bag. Out comes Dr Pepper, potato chips, chocolate, jelly beans, and chocolate chip cookies.

"What about the sandwiches?"

"I changed my mind." She takes a deep breath. "I was thinking about Illinois and how I need to be different there. Grandma won't be with me all the time. The more I think about all the stuff I might have to do, the more I realize I don't know how to do it. Do you know I've never made my own doctor or dentist appointment? I've never sent back a meal at a restaurant. There could be a roach on my salad, and I wouldn't be assertive enough to tell the server. I have to practice this stuff."

I pop two jelly beans into my mouth. "I'm trying to connect the dots. How'd you go from sandwiches to jelly beans?"

"Because I really want junk food, but I know it's not the right choice. I decided I shouldn't care about what the cashier thinks."

"You really care about what the cashier thinks?"

"Stupid, huh?"

"Not stupid. I know it's hard for you, but I didn't know it was that hard."

Eden says. "Maybe you should try to talk me out of eating this stuff, so I can practice being assertive."

"You sure? I don't want to stress you out."

"I'm sure."

I read the label on the cookie bag. "Two cookies have 140 calories!"

"That's not too bad for a treat."

"Nobody stops at two cookies. We'll eat the whole bag, plus you have potato chips and chocolate. And Jessica says chocolate gives you pimples."

"I think that's an old wives' tale."

"What about all the chemicals in this stuff? I can't pronounce half of the ingredients."

Eden takes the cookie bag from me. "That's enough. Good practice, right?"

"You were great," I say.

"Really?"

"You held your ground."

"Also the lady at the register accidentally gave me a dime in change instead of a nickel. So I told her she made a mistake, and I gave her back the dime, and she gave me a nickel. That went okay."

I open the cookies and start eating. "Maybe you could get more practice with the wedding. I know everything is pretty much decided, but I'm talking about little things like the color of fingernail polish. You can make that decision."

"Actually, I made a big decision." She stares at the table while she talks. "I didn't even consult Justin about Las Vegas." She looks into my eyes, which Eden doesn't do very often. She's either practicing her assertiveness, or maybe...maybe she trusts me. "You'll support me, right? No matter what?"

"I'm the junior bridesmaid. Why wouldn't I?"

She blushes. "Because...well..."

"What?"

"Never mind."

"Tell me."

"The family won't like it. It's a big city with crime and drinking and gambling, but we won't do any of that. We're going to Hoover Dam." She opens a can of Dr Pepper.

"Anyway, let's talk about something else. I went to St. Vincent de Paul's thrift store the other day and bought a DVD for us to watch." Of course Catholics have their own chain of thrift stores that raise money for charity. St. Vincent de Paul is the Patron Saint of charities, obviously. "I've always wanted to be invited to one of those slumber parties where girls stay up late, eat junk food, and watch scary movies. But I was never invited. Not once. So I bought *Friday the 13th*."

I'm not supposed to watch R-rated movies, but I'm not going to ruin the bride's one and only slumber party. I'll close my eyes and plug my ears. We finish cleaning up, and as soon as it gets dark, I dump a bunch of pillows in front of the TV, and Eden starts the movie. For the next ninety minutes, my heart pumps at race car speed. I saw *Coraline* a few years ago and had to sleep on the floor of my parents' bedroom for a week. And that was a kids' movie! Obviously *Friday the 13th* is higher on the fear scale. In the movie, these young people are reopening a camp near a beautiful lake. Years before, a boy drowned there because counselors weren't paying attention. One by one, the teens trying to open the camp are murdered, and it turns out the dead boy's mother is killing everyone to prevent the camp from reopening. We watch half the movie with our hands over our eyes. At one point, Eden screams, and then I scream, which makes her scream again.

When the credits roll, I laugh and say, "Nice choice! You pick a movie about a murderer in the woods while we're stuck in the north woods of Minnesota."

Eden says, "I wanted to turn it off fifteen minutes after it started."

"Why didn't you say something?" I hit her with a pillow.

"I didn't want to ruin it for you."

"Eden, it would've been the perfect time for you to practice being assertive."

"Can we sleep with the lights on?" She shuts the blinds on the living room windows.

"Definitely."

"I think we need a distraction, and I'm craving fries. There's a McDonald's on the bypass, right?"

I don't know how she can eat after all the cookies and potato chips, but it's her slumber party, so I change from pajamas back into clothes.

Turns out McDonald's is closed.

Across the highway from McDonald's, squatting on the hillside like a fat king, is Home Supply Station. Brent

Helzinski isn't the only bully in this town. I think about Mom, who can identify the difference in nail grades with a glance, having to work at Home Supply Station with dumb clerks who think *nails* mean *tips of your fingers*.

"Eden, drive to Home Supply Station. I want to pretend it's a Saturday afternoon and see it completely empty. I want to see full shelves with sale stickers and nobody in line waiting to buy things."

"Are you sure?"

"I'm sure."

That's the great thing about Eden. Rather than tell me I'm being childish, she understands. She drives across the highway, parks by the cart corral near the entrance, and turns off the engine.

I stare at the big sign near the door. *Big Savings on Garden Tools!* In an instant I'm reliving that moment when Brent held me under water. It's like I can't get any air. I'm afraid and angry at the same time. I hate this store even more than I hate Brent Helzinski. I despise its TV ads that end with the sound of a train whistle. (Train whistle! Home Supply "Station!" Get it?) I hate its orange-and-green sign and its money-back guarantee.

How can one heart hold so much hate?

"I'm sorry about the store, Mary. It's terrible."

"My great grandfather built our store. I mean literally, brick by brick."

"It makes all of us sad, really, it does. But Grandma says your dad will make good money at the oil job, and he won't work so many hours. Grandma says it's a blessing in disguise."

"Blessings shouldn't come in disguise. Grandma thinks she knows what's best for everyone, and she doesn't. Look at the wedding! She's driving everyone crazy."

"She wants it to be perfect."

"Perfect for who? Her?"

Eden sighs. "Can we go home now?"

"You know my mom might take a job at this stupid store."

"I heard."

I think about Nick and his shoplifting and how Ecuador's economy might be smaller than Home Supply Station's bank account. I think about Jesus yelling at the people who did business in church.

"This place is just another bully kicking around people who work hard. You know who's worse than the bully? The people who shop here. It's like the kids at your school—some of them picked on you, but most stood around and ignored it. That's worse. God, I could scream."

"Maybe you should. Maybe it would help."

I open the window and shout, "I hate you, Home Supply Station! I hope you burn to the ground!"

"Feel better?"

"A little."

I open the door and march closer to the building, past the cart corral, and scream, a long ear-splitting scream like the girls in *Friday the 13th*.

I hear Eden's door open. "Okay, it's good you let all that out, and now you feel better. Let's go."

The scream doesn't empty my rage. It fills up the tank. I pick up a water bottle dumped by the cart corral and throw it as hard as I can. The bottle is light, so it floats a few feet and lands on the pavement. I look around for something else.

"Mary? Please let's go."

"In a minute."

"Get back in the car please, because it's a good idea to get back in the car."

I see a golf-ball-size rock and grab it. I snap my arm back in a wind-up, and just as I'm about to smash the glass entrance of the fat king, I feel a tug on my arm. The rock fires off to the side and hits the light pole. Eden gasps and squeezes my arm tight.

"You of all people should get it!" I yell. "You need to explode more than anyone. Get a rock and throw it. Let's break the windows. They'll never know it was us."

Eden points to the car. She takes a deep breath and says, "Mary Margaret Miller. Get in the car, and I mean it." For the first time, I see Grandma in Eden's face—her wide eyes and the arch of her eyebrows, the way she tilts her head. "And please do it right now if you don't mind."

I snatch my hand away and return to the car, making sure to slam the door hard. Instead of driving straight to my house, she cruises through town. It's like a slideshow of my life: Holmestrand Elementary, Jessica's house, the bronze plaque that lists all the Holmestrand people who died in war, Holmestrand City Hall, Dave's Diner, Hair Affair Salon, Bernquist and Stenski Law Firm, and the empty Miller Family Hardware with its "For Sale" sign.

"Just drive home so we can go to bed," I say.

Instead, Eden turns left and pulls into St. Bridget's parking lot. She stops near the front door and turns off the engine.

"What are you doing?"

"I want to help, but I don't know what to say. Maybe the church doors are open. Would you like to go inside and pray?"

"Praying is like screaming in outer space. Nobody hears you." I've turned on a faucet. The feelings and the words gush. "Go ahead. Tell me I'm a bad Catholic."

"Mary, I think everyone wonders about praying." She takes a deep breath. "I don't even like admitting it out loud, but sometimes I get angry at God."

I give her a sharp look. She's chewing on her thumbnail.

"No matter how angry I get, I know He forgives me."

"News flash, Eden: God isn't listening."

But Eden doesn't look shocked by what I've just said. Instead she quietly says, "I didn't know you feel like that, and I'm sorry." There's no lightning bolt from Heaven, and Eden's not telling me that I'm a bad person, or reminding me that these thoughts are sins, or trying to talk me out of how I feel. She adjusts the rearview mirror and fidgets with the keys. "You should talk to Grandma."

"Hah!"

"I mean it. She left the church for a whole year, and not many people know that."

I'm stunned. "Grandma? The Rosary Queen?"

"You'll have to ask her about it because I think it would help you see that lots of people feel what you're feeling."

"I doubt it."

"Mary, it's bad for your heart to throw rocks at windows and punch boys in the face. I'm not lecturing you about doing that, but I'm saying it makes you feel terrible, and I don't want you to feel terrible."

"So Mom told everyone about Brent. Figures."

"We're your family, and we're not judging you."

I look out the window, so I don't have to see her, and say, "You'd judge if you knew the truth."

"Do you want to tell me the truth?"

I don't.

But I need to. I've been keeping it inside for months and months, and for the first time, I'm more afraid of collapsing under the weight of the secret than what people will think when they know the truth.

I tell her everything I told Nick—how Brent had been picking on me because I'd accidentally hit him during kickball, how he held me under water at the apple-bobbing game, how I smashed his nose with the apple, how we picked on each other for months, how I slugged him in the hall by my locker.

"I want you to guess why I hit Brent," I say.

She thinks for a moment. "I'm guessing you were defending yourself because he threatened you or maybe pushed you or said something truly horrible."

"That's what everyone thinks. You know why? Because Brent is a jerk who's failing half his classes, and his mom is a drunk. But what happened is the bell was about to ring, and Brent walked up to me. Everyone was clearing out, so we were mostly alone. I was expecting him to say something mean, and I was ready. I wasn't even afraid of him anymore. I learned it was pretty easy to take him down with comments about how fat he is. I'd called him a walking sausage, chub muffin, tank, chunky monkey, and Fatzilla." Eden gasps a little, but I continue. "But that day, he didn't say anything mean or try to trip me. He said, 'This is getting stupid. I just want it to stop. So I'll stop if you stop. I'm sorry about the Halloween party. And I'll say I'm sorry for the rest if you say you're sorry.'"

"Was he lying?"

"I don't think so. Everything about him was different. His voice was quiet. His face was serious. I think he was ready to be done with it. And it made me so mad. Madder than I've ever been." I take a deep breath. "So I punched him."

"I don't get it."

"I can't completely explain it, either. But I think I got angry because I didn't want our fight to end."

"I still don't get it."

"In the weirdest way it felt good to be fighting with him."

The car is silent.

"I know it's crazy," I say.

Eden squeezes the steering wheel and thinks. Finally she says, "Maybe you couldn't do anything about Home Supply Station, or your Dad moving away, or switching schools, but fighting with Brent gave you power."

I shrug. "Maybe. Brent's apology set me on fire, so maybe you're right. I guess I needed someone to fight with. I couldn't yell at Mom, but I wanted to. She's been so whiney and annoying, like she's the only one who misses Dad." It's warm in the car, so I roll down the window. I hear the song of crickets and frogs from the tree line next to the church—sounds I don't hear in St. Paul. "You know what? Every single person who's asked me about it—my friends, the principal, Mom, even Father Benson—asked me what Brent did to make me hit him. Every single person. And the truth is he didn't do anything."

"I know your heart is full of kindness, Mary. You're a good person with love in your heart." She does her deep-breathing thing and says, "That's why you're going to apologize before we leave tomorrow."

"No way. Never."

"You'll feel peace. You'll be able to forgive yourself and put it behind you."

"I don't want to see him ever again."

Eden's voice shakes. "You're making me practice being assertive, I guess. You see, I have the keys and the car, and we're not leaving until you make it right by telling that boy you're sorry. It's for you as much as it is for him."

I'm too shocked to argue. I've never heard Eden say something with such strength, but I'm even more surprised by my reaction.

I think Eden is right.

Chapter Twenty-one

There's going to be a wedding in 6 days

B<small>RENT LIVES IN A TINY, SQUARE-SHAPED HOUSE NOT FAR</small> from the bypass that leads to Home Supply Station. The bushes under the windows are brown and dry like stalks of tumbleweed that can't blow away.

"Good luck." Eden rolls down the window. "I'll be here if you need me."

"What if he's not home?"

"Then maybe you can write a letter, but maybe he is home."

Two things are torturing me. First, it's Brent. He's not known for being a kind and forgiving guy. Second, I'm not used to delivering big apologies because I'm always nice to people. I want it over fast.

Brent's mom opens the door and squints against the sunlight. In all the years I've known Brent, I've never seen Mrs. Helzinski at school like the rest of the parents, who volunteer for classroom parties, come to lunch, cheer at games, and browse the science fair. I've only seen her leaving the bar across the street from our store.

"Yeah?" Her voice is gritty like sandpaper.

"Is Brent home?"

She stares with flat-brown eyes. They're Brent's eyes. I can't tell if she's generally unhappy about morning visitors, or if she knows I'm the girl who punched her son. Finally she says, "Just a minute."

As I wait, I say a quick prayer to Dominic Savio, Patron Saint of juvenile delinquents. *Dear Saint Dominic Savio, Here's your chance to show me you're not deaf. Help me get through this.*

Brent presses his face against the screen and blinks in surprise. "What do you want?"

His acne has spread from his forehead down his nose and cheeks. When he scratches his head, his shirt rises and displays a ring of belly.

I spit out the words. "I want to say I'm sorry."

"Sure you are."

"I am. I really am sorry. Really."

He makes a high-pitched voice and mocks me. "Really really really really?" Then he laughs. "You moved. I know you moved because the town stopped smelling like butt when you left."

Since I've been practicing revenge all year, my instinct is to blurt out something mean, or call him "Count Fatula," an insult I'd saved all winter for the right moment. But I'm not going to do that. I'm going to turn the other cheek because the other cheek *can* be turned.

"I was really awful to you most of the year, Brent. And that's not the person I want to be, and I want you to know that I was wrong, and I know I was wrong. So I'm sorry, and I guess I'll just leave now."

But I don't leave. I shift back and forth, waiting for him to offer his forgiveness, so my heart will feel whole, like Eden said.

Brent says, "You came back to tell me you're sorry?"

"I had to take care of some stuff before we move. Saying sorry was one part of it."

He frowns and shrugs. "Okay."

"Okay," I say, still waiting.

"Yeah, well, okay then." He shuts the door. At least it's not a slam.

I don't know what I was expecting. Obviously it wasn't going to be one of those movie-type apologies where I say I'm sorry, and then he says something nice, and we become friends. I wasn't really expecting him to say something overly sweet because he's not like that, but I thought he'd say something more than *okay*. He could've said goodbye or good luck or have fun in your new school.

I guess okay is better than nothing. Okay is as good as it gets.

Eden's in the bathroom at the gas station when I notice a colorful brochure sticking out of her purse. We're still an hour from St. Paul, and she wants to get home before the traffic hits. I see the words Las Vegas across the top of the brochure, so it has to be something about the surprise honeymoon. I pull it out and look at the pictures. It's a gorgeous hotel with palm trees and the biggest pool I've ever seen. Tucked inside is a printout of the trip details, and something catches my eye.

Departure: 9:30 a.m., August 17.

That makes no sense. The wedding is August 19. I read it again and again. *Departure: 9:30 a.m., August 17.* How is that possible?

Slowly I put it together, like a movie where the mystery is explained in flashbacks...Eden sitting on her bed saying she can't take any more of the wedding planning...Eden swearing me to secrecy about the Las Vegas trip...Eden saying she's not going to be eating cake at the wedding...Eden telling me she's dealing with her wedding in her own way...

This trip to Las Vegas isn't just a honeymoon. Eden and Justin are going to elope.

When I see Eden coming back to the car, I shove the brochure and papers back in her purse.

"You sure you don't need to use the bathroom? It's actually clean."

"I'm sure."

Eden drives back to the highway and turns off the radio. "I have a massive headache. Do you mind if it's quiet?"

I mumble no, but I want to ask if this massive headache has anything to do with a massive secret. I can't believe it. Eden wouldn't give up her church wedding. Would she? Eden's not a person who'd hurt Grandma's feelings. But

I'm not the kind of person who would punch a boy in the face, either. And that's exactly what I did.

Still, Eden wouldn't run off and disappoint us. Between our family and Justin's family, there are 400 people coming to the wedding. She wouldn't ruin an event for 400 people.

Would she?

I don't know. I have to put myself in Eden's mind. *Most* people wouldn't flee their own wedding. But for Eden, there are 400 reasons to run away.

Chapter Twenty-two

There's going to be a wedding in 5 days

THE NEXT DAY, WHILE EDEN'S WORKING, I FLIP THROUGH the Patron Saint notebook and count the stars. I give up when I reach 300, because what's the point? The notebook is a time-waster. I stuff it under the bed and get the button Nick made from the nightstand drawer. I run my fingers over the words: Mary Miller Patron Saint for Junior Bridesmaids.

Until yesterday, when I saw the plane tickets, I thought I'd been doing a good job as the junior bridesmaid. Not so good that I'm worthy of being an actual Patron Saint, but pretty good for an inexperienced kid with no adults advising me. Obviously, though, I'm a huge failure—I missed the clues that Eden is going to run from this overly spectacular wedding.

I don't know what to do. If I tell Grandma, she'll go nuclear, and Eden might never speak to me again. If I tell Aunt Maggie or Mom, they'd immediately tell Grandma, and she'd go nuclear, because that's how it works in my family. Grandma is the queen. Even if I convince Eden to stay in St. Paul and get married, the wedding might be a disaster, and it would be my fault. She might faint or puke, or she might panic and leave poor Justin at the altar.

I could look for the Patron Saint for eloping couples, if there is such a person, but why bother? The saints either don't listen or don't care.

There aren't any good options—just bad options and worse options.

I squeeze Nick's button and wonder what he'd say about this mess. I look out the window. He's not in his driveway, but maybe he's inside. I don't want Eden to come home and see the button, but I want to keep it. I'm never going to throw it away. I decide to put it in the rosary box. I get the little key from the dresser, open the suitcase lock, and put the rosary box on the bed. Out of habit, I send one final plea to Blessed Imelda. *Dear Holy Blessed Imelda, show me the universe isn't on autopilot. Please.*

I lift the Pope Francis prayer card. My heart nearly stops beating.

The Communion wafer is gone.

Gone!

My feet move in a blur—down the stairs, out the door, across the lawn. I bang on Nick's door and wait for what seems like forever. He opens the door and smiles. "Guess what? My dad got me a new skateboard, so now I have two." He looks at me. "What's wrong?"

I sit on his front step and pull my knees to my chest. "I don't even know what to say. It's so weird."

He sits down, too. "Good weird? Bad weird?"

"There was a Communion wafer in my rosary box, and it's gone."

"Um . . . okay."

"Gone! It just disappeared."

"Am I missing some information?"

"I think it's a miracle," I whisper. My hands are shaking. "It's a long story, Nick, and you have to understand Communion and all that, but trust me. It's miraculous."

"I'm still missing some information here."

"I've had this chewed-up piece of Communion wafer,

which is the Body of Christ, by the way, in my rosary box, and I've been praying to Blessed Imelda—"

"Who?"

"She's the Patron Saint of Communion. I've been praying to her to help me get rid of this wafer because it's sacred. You can't throw it away. So it's been in my rosary box for weeks, and now it's gone."

Nick's face twists like he's thinking hard. "Maybe it disintegrated."

"In a few weeks?"

"Maybe ants ate it."

"Impossible. Bugs couldn't get into that box."

"Maggots could, I think."

"No." I cross my arms. "They couldn't."

"Luke probably took it."

"I hid it in my suitcase, one of those with the little lock and key on the zipper. It was locked, and I hid the key in the dresser." I take a breath and say, "There's no explanation."

"There must be an explanation, Mary. I'm sorry, but things don't just disappear."

"Exactly! Things don't just disappear. That's why it's a miracle." I stare at him, but Nick looks away. "What? You don't believe me?"

"Faith is belief without evidence, right? I believe you have faith, so yes, I believe you."

"That's a weird way of saying it." I'm waiting for him to believe it, to feel it like I feel it. But he looks at his shoes. I cross my arms and say, "Nobody in your family or your church believes in miracles? Your culture?"

"I once read that Vietnam is the least traditionally religious country of any in the world. Doesn't matter, though, because I'm not from Vietnam. I'm from St. Paul, Minnesota. My parents were born in St. Paul, Minnesota. My grandparents are the last people in my family to set foot in Vietnam, and only one of them is still alive."

"Oh, so nobody in Vietnam is Christian? Nobody?"

"A lot of people are Buddhist, but that religion is more about enlightenment."

He makes me so mad. No matter what I say, he has something smarter. "Sorry. I haven't spent my whole life studying the world's religions."

"Don't get mad." He looks surprised I'm upset. "I just don't believe in miracles. I believe in science."

"It's faith, not science. Your heart belongs in faith. Otherwise we'd be people with brains and logic and nothing else. No emotion."

"Even emotion comes from your brain, not your heart. What we feel is caused by chemicals in the brain."

I haven't been this mad at a boy since Brent Helzinski. I don't say anything else because I'll end up yelling. Nick stays quiet, too. We sit on the step, me with my arms crossed, him staring at his shoes.

When Grandma's car pulls up to the house, I've never been happier to see her and have her yell at me to stop dilly dallying and come inside. I don't want to spend one more second with Mr. Intellectual. I jump off the step like I'd been sitting on a spring and run to the house, making sure the door slams with a bang.

I sink into the living room couch and try not to think about Nick and whether ants were in my rosary box feasting on the Body of Christ. Is that even possible?

I hear Grandma telling Luke we need a few minutes alone. She comes to the living room, crosses her arms, and speaks with a low voice. "Mary, come to the kitchen with me. We're overdue for a talk."

Her laser eyes shoot through me, and I think my spine might melt. I follow her to the kitchen, slump in a chair, and try to figure out what I've done. Maybe the Home Supply Station had cameras in the parking lot, and the cameras caught me throwing the rock, and the police tracked Eden's car, and Grandma knows.

"I'm very disappointed in you, Mary."

"Why?"

There's something about Grandma's face. The way she's raising her eyebrow, the way her lips press together. And it hits me: Blessed Imelda isn't the miracle-maker.

Grandma took the Communion wafer!

"Luke told me everything."

I'm stunned. It takes me a moment to find my voice. "Did he tell you it's not my fault? Because it's not my fault."

Grandma's eyes grow wide. "Mary Margaret Miller, if you keep a secret about something wrong, then you are also wrong."

Her words are supposed to make me feel guilty, but they just make me mad. It's totally unfair. *This* is what Mom's trying to avoid with her truth-stretching. I kind of get it.

"Believe me," Grandma continues, "I plan to have words with your mother as soon as the wedding is over. I don't want to create problems before Eden's special day."

I take a deep breath and say, "That's why Mom didn't tell you. Because you'd have words. Lots of words."

"Oh, I have more words than you can imagine!"

Luke opens the door. "Grandma, are we playing Monopoly?"

"Sure. You set up the board. I'll be there in a few minutes."

When Luke leaves, Grandma sits next to me and sighs. "That poor boy. He's been suffering under the weight of this secret all summer."

"Luke's been suffering? He gave the wafer and all his suffering to *me*." And I realize, I am relieved. At least the wafer is no longer in its hiding place. Then the relief turns upside down. "Wait a minute. How'd you know where I put it?"

"I can read my granddaughters easier than a picture book." Ha! She must be reading Eden in a different language, because she's clueless about Eden's dream wedding. She says, "I knew you wouldn't toss it. I knew you'd try to preserve the integrity of Communion, and I'd seen your rosary box when I was putting away laundry. When I went up there yesterday and it was gone, I knew you'd hidden it. And I was meeting with Father Owens that night, so it was critical I get it to him so he could handle it properly."

"So you looked through my stuff?"

"How else was I going to find it? I don't have X-ray vision! I saw the suitcase. It was locked, and I figured the little key was somewhere nearby, and it was. I found it in the dresser. Problem solved." Grandma looks impressed with herself.

I don't care about her spine-melting look. "Grandma, you totally violated my privacy. And Eden's, too!"

"It couldn't wait. It's a long trip from Holmestrand to St. Paul. What if you died in a car accident? You'd have died in a state of sin!"

"You could have called."

"That's not the kind of thing you discuss on the phone. Completely inappropriate."

"So is going through our stuff. That's not appropriate."

"If you had told me, I wouldn't have needed to go through your things."

Here's where I'm supposed to give up, but I'm not going to. I take a deep breath and blow it slowly through my lips, just like Eden. "Grandma, nobody tells you things because you either ignore them or freak out and make everybody feel bad."

I stare at the table and wait for the explosion. But it's quiet, so finally I raise my eyes. Grandma is looking at her clasped hands. I say, "I get it. I should've taken the wafer to Father Owens that morning. But I didn't want Mom in trouble or Luke in trouble or me in trouble. I would've ended up in Confession, and I hate Confession."

"That's ridiculous. Why would you hate Confession?"

"I'm supposed to be the good kid. I have an award to prove it."

She shakes her head. "A good kid? Sure. But not a perfect kid. Father Owens knows more than anyone that nobody is perfect. He hears the worst of the worst—probably never anything quite like our Communion problem, but he's a priest, and it's his job to hear the awful things people do."

"But I don't do awful things. Not usually. I mean, I hit Brent Helzinski and I kept a bad secret." I realize I'm still keeping a bad secret: Eden's secret. I should tell Grandma.

But that's what Mom or Aunt Maggie would do. They'd tiptoe around the problem. I need to talk to Eden. Not Grandma. Not Justin.

Grandma interrupts my thoughts. "Confession is important because it's a way to pray for forgiveness."

"I don't need a priest to help me pray. Besides, I've

been praying to Blessed Imelda for a miracle with this Communion wafer, and it's been a huge waste of time."

Grandma squeezes my hands. "Has it?"

"Yes!"

"Seems to me your prayer was answered. Luke told me, and I took care of it."

"That's not a miracle. That's just you fixing a problem. Patron Saints are a complete and total waste of time."

"What do you think a miracle looks and sounds like? Blinding light from above? Harp music? Miracles happen all around us every single day, and we don't even notice. Prayers are never wasted. Besides, saints only join us in praying to God. They're simply prayer *assistants*. God is the boss. Saints are secretaries. Jesus is second in command, and Mary...well, she's like the director of public relations. Prayers are like memos."

My mouth drops open. "Are you comparing Heaven to an office?"

"It's the best I could do on the spot." She crosses her arms. "You think I don't understand, but I do. When your grandfather had his accident, I prayed for years that he'd get better. And when he got worse, I prayed that he'd live. Then he died. I was heartbroken and furious. I stopped going to church for an entire year." She pauses, then waves her hand like she's removing the bad feelings in the air. "Sad talk doesn't help anyone with anything, does it? I'll make you a sandwich."

"I don't want a sandwich. I want to know why you went back."

Grandma gets ham and mayo from the refrigerator. "I need it. I need the rituals, the community, and the sense of love. I don't know more about God and prayer than I did when I was a little girl. But I do know that saints inspire me. Jesus makes me feel whole. I don't think God took my husband to punish me. We're human, so we'll never understand. I gave up trying to understand it and focused on accepting it."

I sigh. "Basically, you're telling me it is what it is."

"Why, Mary!" Grandma looks so pleased. "That's very wise."

She puts the sandwich in front of me. I take a bite, and I have to admit it goes down pretty well. Grandma squeezes my shoulder and sits next to me. "You've always been the feisty one. Eden could learn a thing or two from you." My mouth is full of sandwich, so I can't respond. "You know, I should have forced Eden to take charge of this wedding. It would've helped with her…issues. I knew she wouldn't get the wedding of her dreams if I didn't advocate for her, but I can't help wondering if I should've forced her to say, 'I want a beautiful dress. I want a real band.'"

I cough bread crumbs. The door opens, and Luke says, "I've been waiting forever. Can we play now?"

"Absolutely." Grandma tugs my arm. "You, too."

"No thanks. I'm tired."

"If you don't want to play, then you can watch. My sofa is very, very comfortable."

She won't take no for an answer, so I pick up my sandwich and follow them to Grandma's side of the house. They sit at the table, but I stop in the doorway. I really don't want to play Monopoly. I *am* tired.

Mom would sit down and play. Aunt Maggie would sit down and play. So would Eden. Not me. "I'm tired. I'm not going to play."

"Come on Mary," Luke says. "I'm going to be the little car. You can be the hat."

"Don't be ridiculous." Grandma pats the seat next to her. "You're young and full of energy."

"No." My voice shakes a little. "I'm going to take a nap."

Grandma blinks. "Mary—"

"I don't want to play. I really, really, really don't want to play."

Luke looks shocked. I wait for Grandma's spine-melting stare, but she just sighs. "Mary Margaret Miller. You most definitely are the feisty one."

Chapter Twenty-three

There's going to be a wedding in **3** days

THE PROBLEM WITH THE UNFINISHED SECTION OF THE Grand Canyon puzzle is the color. I can't sort the pieces because there's beige, beige, beige, and a beigier shade of beige, and the variation in the shapes is too subtle for my eyes. For every twenty pieces I try to press together, I get maybe one to fit. My neck hurts from leaning forward, and my fingers are stiff.

I look out the window to see if Eden's car has returned. She's been either at work, or with Justin for the past two days. It's nearly midnight, and she's still not home. Maybe she suspects I'm on to her plot. I remember what she said about being quiet and paying attention and noticing things other people don't see.

If I don't do something, Eden and Justin will be on a plane tomorrow morning. Grandma went crazy with the wedding plans, but it's not fair for Eden to run off. Sure, Grandma did everything wrong, but it's too late to fix. It's not fair to run away. People can't be uninvited. The dress can't be sent back.

It is what it is.

I call Eden again and leave another voicemail. "Hey Eden. It's me again. Just calling to see if you got my texts and voicemail messages. " If I wasn't so stressed, I'd laugh at myself, because I sound like my mom. She'll text me to see if I read her e-mail and then leave me a voicemail to see if I got her text about her e-mail.

I go back to the puzzle. For another hour, I try to connect the walls of the Grand Canyon. Finally I hear a car door and muffled voices. It's Eden and Justin walking hand-in-hand toward the house. I race downstairs and get to the porch just as they're getting comfortable on the wicker sofa.

"Where have you been?" Justin and Eden laugh, but I don't think it's funny. "I've been waiting all night, and you didn't respond to my messages."

"My phone died and I didn't have my phone charger with me," Eden says. "I'm sorry. Is everything okay?"

"No. Everything is not okay."

"What? What happened?" Eden sounds panicked, and I'm fine with letting her feel that way. I draw out the moment and then say, "I know the truth, Eden. And what you're doing is wrong. Grandma's spent a fortune on this wedding, and I know you don't like the way it's turned out, but that's too bad."

Justin puts his arm around Eden and says, "What's going on?"

I keep my eyes locked on Eden. "I saw the travel stuff in your purse, and I know it's not some surprise honeymoon. You're eloping."

"What's she talking about?" Justin asks.

"What's the plan, Eden?" I'm on a roll. "Did you think you could get him to the airport and explain everything once you got there?"

Eden's face is blank. "I have no idea what you're talking about."

"I saw the tickets. Your flight leaves for Las Vegas tomorrow. That makes it hard to get married in St. Paul on Saturday, doesn't it?"

"Tickets to Las Vegas?" Justin asks.

Eden seems lost. Her voice is nearly a whisper. "As a surprise for you, I bought a Las Vegas vacation package for our honeymoon. But we leave the morning after the wedding."

"No you don't. You leave tomorrow. That's August seventeenth." I have a sinking feeling. Am I wrong? Could I have possibly developed a reading disorder?

Eden opens her purse and digs out the papers. It's dark, so she holds them close to her face, and gasps. "I'm so stupid! Oh my God, how could I be so stupid? I got the dates wrong. I remember the best deal was for August 17, and I was going to pay the extra amount to go the day after the wedding, but I was running late for work and clicked through everything so fast … God, I'm an idiot."

Eden drops her head in her hands. Justin rubs her back. "Don't say that about yourself. I don't know exactly what's going on, but we'll fix it, ok?"

I lean against the door. "So you aren't planning to elope?"

"Of course not!" Eden has tears in her eyes. "How could you think I would do that to Grandma? To my family? You think I would just disappear without a word to anyone?"

"I'm sorry. I don't think that—"

"You did. That's what you thought."

"It's just a misunderstanding," Justin says.

"Eden," I say, "I thought maybe you were taking control to make this wedding your own. That one night you sat on your bed and said you couldn't take any more. You even said you won't be eating cake at the wedding."

"Because I'll be too nervous. That's all I meant."

"In Holmestrand it sounded like—"

"Like I was nervous? Of course I'm nervous. That doesn't mean I'd do something deceitful and cruel."

The door opens. It's Uncle Will. "What's going on out here?" He runs his hand through his rumpled hair.

The three of us say, "Nothing."

"Well, it's a pretty loud bunch of nothing." He leans forward and squints at Eden. "Are you crying?" Then he says to Justin, "What did you do?"

"Nothing, sir!"

"It wasn't Justin," I say. "It was me. I screwed up. I made a mistake, and I said something mean to Eden."

Eden sniffles and waves the papers with the trip information. "No. I made the mistake."

"No. It was me. I was wrong."

"I shouldn't have rushed through my first vacation purchase."

"I shouldn't have taken something out of your purse."

"Thankfully you did. Maybe we can fix it."

"Taken what? Fix what?" Uncle Will says.

Grandma's voice comes from the darkness. "Fix what? Taken what?"

Justin says, "We'll call the airline, and we'll explain, and even if we have to pay extra, we'll make it work."

"Pay extra for what?" Uncle Will says.

"Make what work?" Grandma says.

Eden sighs. "It's a long story."

"Well, we're all up now," Grandma says. "Come inside. I'll make sandwiches and you can tell us all about it."

I say, "We'll be right there." Uncle Will and Justin follow Grandma, and I shut the door so they can't hear us. "Eden, I'm really, really sorry. I feel stupid."

Eden sighs. "You're not stupid. I can see how you connected the dots. But why didn't you ask me right away?"

I swallow and think. "Because you had a headache." As soon as I say it, I know it sounds ridiculous. "Because... I don't know."

"This trumped a headache, definitely."

"We're such a close family." I shrug and stare at my feet. "But sometimes it's still hard to talk about stuff."

"I know, but I thought you and I were different. We're not Grandma. We're not our moms. We're *us*."

Her words make me happy. I'm glad we're in the darkness of the porch, because I'm blushing. And if I'm blushing, Eden's probably purple. I smile and say, "You're right. We are different."

Eden laughs a little. "Thank God."

We do a sign of the cross at the same time and go inside for sandwiches.

Chapter Twenty-four

There's going to be a wedding in 1 day

"Bless Us Lord And These Gifts Amen."

Uncle Will starts passing dishes—corned beef and cabbage, soda bread, and boxty, which is an Irish potato pancake.

"Will, I think you've outdone yourself," Dad says. "This smells and looks delicious." He hands the basket of soda bread to Justin, who takes a small piece and passes it to Grandma, who takes an even smaller piece and says, "Normally I say Irish meals have no flavor, but this dinner is well seasoned with prewedding jitters." She laughs while Uncle Will glares at her.

"Mother!" Aunt Maggie shakes her head.

Nobody else laughs. We're tired.

Mom and Dad arrived late last night. This morning, Grandma woke everyone early and handed out to-do lists. We spent the day checking off the tasks. Aunt Maggie and I bought back-up pairs of pantyhose in case we get runs. Mom went to the flower shop to personally inspect the corsages. Dad figured out how to set Aunt Maggie's slideshow to music. When Grandma found out Uncle Will planned to wear white socks with his tuxedo, she took him shopping to make sure he got black dress socks—not dark blue, not gray, not brown. Black. And that was just before noon.

Grandma says, "Actually, I'm enjoying this boxty. I'm saying so because it's true, and it's important to tell the truth." Grandma looks at Mom as she says it, but Mom doesn't notice. She's helping Luke cut a piece of corned beef.

"Why are we having more cabbage when we know for a fact that Justin doesn't like cabbage?" Luke asks.

"I like cabbage." Justin turns his usual shade of red. "Especially this cabbage. It's quite delicious."

I nudge Luke. "I think you're the one who doesn't like cabbage."

"If you don't like cabbage, Luke, you should just say so," Grandma says. "It's important to tell the truth."

"I don't like cabbage," he says.

"See? Telling the truth is easy. And important," Grandma says.

Eden looks at me like, *What's going on?* I just shake my head and roll my eyes. Then Dad steps in. "Speaking of food, I brought a treat."

Mom pats Luke's head. "You'll love this."

"You know how we thought we'd never find restaurant pie as good as Dave's Diner in Holmestrand? Well, your mother and I discovered a café about 30 miles from my job, and the pie is the best we've ever had."

Mom interrupts. "Not as good as Grandma's pie."

"That's why I said *restaurant* pie. If Grandma sold pies in Holmestrand, she'd put poor Dave out of business." Grandma beams a smile as wide as the Grand Canyon. "My point is we drove out of the way yesterday to get a pie to share with you all."

"How nice!" Grandma says.

Uncle Will smiles. Luke rubs his stomach like he can't wait. Justin looks relieved we're talking about something other than cabbage. When it comes to changing the mood at the dinner table, Dad's a champ. Just when I'm about to relax, Luke's words scramble my insides. "Can we invite Nick over for pie?"

I freeze, but Grandma says, "Sure."

Luke turns to me. "Are you fighting with him? Because when we drove up you were on his front step and you looked super mad and then you came inside and slammed the door real hard."

My face burns.

"That's not your business," Dad says. "You need to respect Mary's privacy."

"Unless someone's soul is at stake," Grandma replies, "and you have to look through their things. Then it's an entirely different story. Wouldn't you agree, Mary?"

Luke says, "Mary should apologize."

"There will be no apologies until this wedding is over." Grandma stares at Mom. "Then, believe me, there will be overdue apologies."

Justin looks confused. The poor guy needs a special family dictionary to understand what we're *really* saying.

"Mary should apologize right now," Luke says. "I don't think she's friends with Nick anymore."

I want Dad to pull another rabbit out of his hat and change the subject, but Uncle Will takes over and tells Dad that Nick charges too much for yard work, then Grandma lists off reasons why Nick's a sweet kid, then Luke starts in with apology demands. I'm in quicksand.

"I'd like to stop talking about this." Everyone goes silent, not because the voice is loud or rude, but because it's Eden. She interrupted with forceful words. Eden! She looks at me, clears her throat, and says, "My wedding is tomorrow and I'd like to stop talking about this and perhaps I'd like a piece of that pie."

Of course she blushes, but she keeps her eyes steady. Then she smiles at me. I'd consider it the perfect moment, except for this: I'm not sure if Nick is friends with me anymore.

Part Three

It's Time for a Wedding

There's going to be a wedding today

WITH A SWIRL OF A BLACK CAPE, THE STYLIST REVEALS
Eden the bride. Grandma, Aunt Maggie, and Mom gasp. I
touch her hair, wondering if it feels like a ribbon, because
that's how it looks. But it's not silky, it's sticky. Today's
hair is for photographs, not fingers.

Eden's beautiful, but it's not a movie makeover. She
didn't transform from ugly duckling with brown-framed
glasses to stunning beauty because of a curling iron and
lipstick. It's still Eden, still wearing glasses. She's always
been beautiful.

"You all look stunning," the stylist says. "What a gorgeous family!"

"I happen to agree," Grandma says with a big smile.

My hair is tucked into a French twist. Mom's hair is in a bun. Grandma and Aunt Maggie's short hair is curled and sprayed into place. I'm wearing makeup, too, even lipstick. Mom and Grandma told the stylist lipstick is okay as long as it's not flaming red. With this makeup and hair, I look like I'm fifteen, maybe even sixteen.

I wonder what Nick would think.

After the salon, Eden and I go home while Grandma, Mom, and Aunt Maggie head to the church to inspect the preparations. The plan is for Eden and me to change at the church so we don't scrunch our dresses in the car. Then there's the ceremony, then we take pictures, then we have the dinner and the dance. We're supposed to relax until they come back from the church and pick us up, but my nerves are on fire. I can't imagine how Eden's feeling. She keeps doing her breathing thing, saying, "We have to finish the puzzle. We have to."

"It's not a big deal."

"It is a big deal to me. I'm doing a transference. That's what they call it in my support group. I'm taking real anxiety about the wedding and transferring it to something trivial. It's not the best coping skill, but at this point, who cares?"

Since this is my last day on junior-bridesmaid duty, I say, "Okay. Let's do this thing." I did a good job with the beige center, but there's still an opening the size of a coaster. Now it's a matter of detecting the tiniest differences in shape. This is where Eden shines. She quickly narrows the space to a few pieces.

I hear the front door open and Grandma's voice. I look at the clock and say, "It's time to go, and you know what Grandma's like."

Eden frowns. "I think we're short one piece."

"Are you sure?"

Eden connects the last few pieces and sure enough, there's one piece missing.

"Girls!" Grandma calls. "Let's go!"

"What'd I tell you? She's a walking clock."

Eden says, "She's not going to leave without me today."

"Looks who's becoming a troublemaker!"

She smiles and says, "Speaking of making trouble, I have a plan. We need to talk."

"What on earth are you girls doing?" Aunt Maggie stands in the doorway with her hands on her hips.

"Sorry, Mom. We have to find the last piece. It's got to be here," Eden says, dropping to her knees in search of that last piece.

"We'll find it later. Let's go."

"I can't. I have to finish the puzzle. I can't leave with one piece missing."

She lays flat on her stomach, creeps up to the bed, and presses her face against the mattress so she can stretch her arm all the way under the bed. Her anxiety must really be getting out of control. The pearl-covered comb falls out of Eden's hair. This transference thing really isn't such a great idea. She's going to ruin her hair and makeup.

Aunt Maggie huffs and puffs. "Eden Mary Collins! Get off the floor!"

Eden grunts a few times, then stands with her arm in the air and a huge smile on her face. "Found it!"

I pick up the comb so I can reattach it, but the comb is broken. Eden opens her palm to reveal the last tiny piece. "You should do the honors."

I shake my head. "No, you should. You're the bride."

"You've been the best junior bridesmaid ever. You do it."

"This is ridiculous! We need to leave now." Aunt Maggie sounds like Grandma. "It's a puzzle, for goodness sake."

"Mary, let's explain to Mom why this is important." Eden looks at me like we planned a speech together, but I'm not sure about my part. I say, "This puzzle was really hard."

Eden sighs. "Mom, we opened this box in June and dumped 5,000 puzzle pieces on this table. Their shapes and sizes are nearly identical. There are only a few distinct colors. We spent hours shuffling and sorting and studying the picture on the box. We had to perfectly match *5,000* individual pieces." Eden holds the final piece in the air. "This is the last piece."

Aunt Maggie says, "Fine. Please put the last piece in the puzzle."

As Eden hands me the last piece of the puzzle, I add a completely unhelpful thought. "Eden and I have been doing puzzles ever since I can remember, Aunt Maggie. This could be the last one we ever do together."

Eden and Aunt Maggie burst into tears at the same moment. Aunt Maggie wails, "My baby girl!" She grabs both of us into a three-way hug. "I'm so proud of you, honey. I'm proud of both of you. I'm the luckiest mom and aunt in the world." Eden and Aunt Maggie explode into full-on sobs, the kind of crying with weird noises and snot.

We pull apart when Grandma steps into the room. Immediately I see the streaks of mascara and makeup on Aunt Maggie and Eden's faces. Grandma gasps and says, "What in the world happened?"

In the mirror I see my face, too. Since our faces were

pressed together, I've got black streaks on cheeks, too. "Oh, no!"

"I'll call the salon," Grandma says. "They can—"

"There's no time." Aunt Maggie takes tissues from the desk and wipes up Eden's face.

"Do I look okay?" Eden asks.

Aunt Maggie kisses her forehead. "Beautiful."

"I can't do this if I look terrible. Do I look terrible? Oh God, I look terrible, don't I?"

"Eden, listen." Grandma's voice is firm. "In all honesty that makeup covered up your beauty. Your crying saved the day."

In my family, we often say things we don't mean, but this time Grandma means every word. I can tell. Eden blows her nose and studies herself in the mirror. Her eyes are red from crying, and her face is red from the tissue scrubbing. Grandma smooths the side of Eden's head where the comb had been.

"Thanks, Grandma," Eden whispers. "Thanks for everything."

This comment makes Grandma cry, and in seconds her makeup is a mess. Now Aunt Maggie has to clean up Grandma's face, too.

"Eden," I say, "This is our moment." I hold up the final

piece of the puzzle and snap it into place. Eden smiles and gives me a thumbs-up.

The princess dress is heavy, and the lace makes my shoulders itch. It's hot in the church's changing room. I'm starting to sweat, which makes the itching worse. I sniff my armpits. Thankfully, they still smell like my powder-fresh deodorant. I lift the dress to scratch my calf, and my nails pierce the fabric and create an instant hole.

"Where'd Grandma put the extra panty hose?"

"She packed a duffle bag. It's by the door."

There's a partition breaking the space into two dressing areas. I step past it and look through the duffle bag until I find the panty hose. When I turn around, I see Eden leaning against the wall, still wearing her button-down shirt and yoga pants.

"Why aren't you dressed?"

"The party can't start without me, right?"

She's sweating. I take tissues from a table in the corner and wipe her forehead. "Do you want a drink of water?"

"Yes, please."

There are two bottles of water in the duffle bag, plus

Band-Aids, protein bars, Tums, tweezers, lip balm, safety pins, breath mints, a sewing kit, aspirin, hair spray, and *more*. I pull out a roll of duct tape. "Check this out!"

Eden takes the water from me. "Remember at the house when I said I have a plan?"

My heart jumps. "Please tell me you're not changing your mind."

"I'm not changing my mind about the wedding." She bites her lip. "But I am changing my mind about something else, and I hope and pray you'll help me."

This doesn't sound good at all. "What is it?"

"I don't want to embarrass you."

Now it *really* doesn't sound good. "Just tell me."

There's a knock at the door, and Grandma says, "Can I come in? I forgot to tell you something very important. Extremely important."

"It's not a good time," I shout. "Can you just tell us?"

"It's extremely important that you don't lock your knees." I mouth the word *what?* at Eden, who shrugs. Through the door, Grandma says, "Bend your knees a little. If you keep your legs completely straight, you'll faint."

I whisper to Eden, "What's she talking about?"

"Thanks, Grandma!" she shouts.

I open the package of panty hose, but Eden tugs on my

arm. "Mary, I need your help. I want to wear the princess dress."

I laugh, but she doesn't. So I say, "It's too late. We can't get another dress now. It's impossible."

Eden bites her lip. "I know. There's no way to get another dress." She looks at her wedding dress and then looks back at me.

"No way!" I gulp. "I can't wear your dress. You can't be serious. Are you? Are you really serious?" She looks at me with pleading eyes and starts chewing on her freshly painted thumbnail. "Of course you're serious. I…I…" I'm stammering.

I can't wear a wedding dress! It's probably illegal for a thirteen-year-old to wear one, and if it's not, it should be! But Patron Saints make huge sacrifices, and wearing a wedding dress isn't like dying for Communion or being tortured. Eden looks so sincere and hopeful. I can probably handle it for her. "Okay. If that's what you want, I will. I will wear your wedding dress."

She pulls me into her arms and squeezes. Her hair feels sticky against my face. "You're the best junior bridesmaid ever."

"A Patron Saint for junior bridesmaids," I say. "You can petition the bishop and get the process going."

She smiles and helps me out of the dress. She disappears behind the partition, and I step into the wedding dress and wait for Eden to close the zipper. It's a simple dress with a narrow skirt, beads on the neckline, and a short train. Bonus that it doesn't itch.

Eden steps in front of me wearing the princess dress. On me, the dress looked—how did the lady in the changing room describe it? Over the top?—but it's different on her. It seems *right*. "You're stunning," I say.

"So are you."

"Grandma is going to have words for us." I laugh. I can't help it.

"She will, but it'll be too late."

There's a knock at the door. "Everything okay?" It's Uncle Will.

"Now or never." I open the door.

Uncle Will blinks in surprise. His eyes sweep side to side. Then he throws his head back and laughs. "Eden Mary Collins! You pick today to let your rebellious Irish side escape?" He shakes his head. "That's fine by me."

Justin's brother Joshua peeks over Uncle Will's shoulder. "This will make for some interesting photos."

Uncle Will winks at me and says, "You're a champ."

My shrug causes the strap on my left shoulder to slip down. I make a mental note to stop shrugging. The music starts, and I walk down the aisle, arm in arm with Joshua, without any expression on my face. I don't look side to side, because if I see the reactions, I'll panic or crack up laughing or both. So I stare over the heads of Justin and Father Owens, nearly to the ceiling. Even with the loud organ music, I hear some gasps and some coughing and a few giggles. I hear Luke squeal, "She's too young to get married!" and Mom shushing him.

When I reach the front of the church, the music changes from soft as tiptoes to a bold march. Everyone stands as the cotton-candy bride, without makeup or the pearl-covered comb, glides toward the front of the church with her father. Justin beams. His eyes seem locked on hers, and I don't think he's paying attention to the dress. Eden's face is pale. She's either so nervous that she drained every shade of red, or she's actually okay. Maybe even happy.

Uncle Will kisses her cheek. Then Justin, Eden, Joshua, and I face Father Owens, who clears his throat and shifts on his feet. I've never seen a speechless priest before. Usually they're loaded with words, and if they absolutely can't think of something, they recite a prayer. Father

Owens coughs a couple of times. I lean toward Eden and say, "Don't lock your knees. Tell Justin." Eden whispers to Justin, who whispers to Joshua.

Finally Father Owen says, "Today we celebrate the marriage of Eden Mary Collins and Justin Joseph Jackson."

I can't look at Grandma, or even my parents, so I stare at the big pink bow on Eden's butt. I tell myself over and over *Don't lock your knees* until I hear Father Owens say, "If anyone here objects to this marriage, you should speak now or forever hold your peace."

And nobody speaks.

Chapter Twenty-six

There's going to be a reception tonight

ADULTS ARE HILARIOUS. I'M HUGGED BY PROBABLY 100 people, and not one of them asks why I'm wearing the wedding dress. They say things like, "What a unique ceremony," and "It's a wedding I'll never forget!" and "My, times are changing!" Nobody says we're crazy. Either people never say what they mean, or it's not a big deal. Only the photographer raises an eyebrow and sighs as she shuffles us in various poses. I can't wait to show the pictures to Jessica. She won't believe this story without proof. I watch the videographer in the back of the room and wonder if he'll put us on YouTube. I hope we don't go viral. The new-kid-in-school thing is going to be hard enough without a million YouTube views.

As the guests find their tables, I inspect the ice sculpture. The faces don't look anything like Eden and Justin. The sculpture looks more like one half of Mount Rushmore. I've got to keep Luke away, because the first thing he'll do is get his tongue stuck on the ice. There's a tug on my arm.

It's Grandma with full-on laser eyes. I try to back up, but she doesn't let go. She shakes her head and says, "I'm beginning to think I'm the only normal person in this family."

"It's like you said the other night. Eden needs to be assertive, and I guess she's trying. That's good, right?"

"Mary Margaret Miller! Why in the world would you say this is good?"

"Because that's the dress she really wanted? So she made a last-minute decision? And she looks pretty?" I'm answering in questions instead of saying what I really mean. I try again. "She does look pretty. And she's happy, so I'm happy, and you should be happy, too."

Grandma throws her hands up in exasperation as she walks away. "If she wanted that dress, all she had to do was say so." She turns around and points at me. "Shoes."

"What?"

"You forgot to switch shoes." Sure enough, I'm still wearing my pastel-pink shoes, and Eden must be in her white heels.

Grandma wiggles through a crowd of people and hugs cousin Bridget.

That could've gone *a lot* worse.

Then it does get worse—Mom shows up. She stands between me and the sculpture with her arms crossed against the blue silk jacket. "What's going on? Grandma has been hostile from the moment I walked in the house. Did you tell her about Luke's Communion?"

I don't want the dark circles to come back, and I don't want to argue at the wedding, but I can't swallow my words anymore. "That's your question? You're not wondering why I'm wearing a *wedding dress?*"

"Your tone is rude, and I don't like it."

"I'm wearing a wedding dress!"

"That's the least of my concerns. I need to know—"

"Mom! Your twelve-year-old daughter is wearing a wedding dress, and you're more concerned about whether Grandma's mad."

She rolls her eyes. "It's not like you actually got married."

I want to look confident, so I cross my arms, but the straps fall off my shoulders again. I pull them back up as gracefully as possible. "It's not fair for you to ask me to keep your secrets. I don't want to do it anymore."

"It's not like a *forever* secret. It's temporary, just until things calm down."

"She knows."

Mom's shoulders droop. "Who told her? You? Uncle Will?" The stress of this conversation is almost as bad as wedding stress. I'm sweaty and tired and hungry. I remind myself to bend my knees. She repeats her words. "Who told her?"

"Luke told her. He did the right thing. He was brave." I tug on the shoulder straps. "And if I'm brave enough to wear Eden's dress in front of 400 people just so she can wear the dress of her dreams, then you can talk to Grandma about Luke's Communion."

Mom's eyes blink like she's in shock.

"It's not as hard as you think. Trust me. I've had a lot of experience over the past few days."

"Well, I guess I deserve that." Her face softens. "I'm sorry. I've missed you so much. We need a new start, all of us." She hugs me.

"I miss you, too."

She tucks a loose strand of hair behind my ear. "I think it's time for us to sit down for dinner. Don't worry about your toast. You'll be great, honey."

My toast? I nearly tip out of my shoes. I completely forgot about having to give a toast. With all the drama in Holmestrand and the missing Communion wafer and Eden's plane tickets, I blocked out the most nerve-racking part of my bridesmaid duties. I grab Mom's arm. "Don't go! I forgot. What should I say?"

"But you were working on it that day we talked on the phone."

"Everything went crazy, and I forgot."

"Mary, it's a pretty big thing to forget."

I rub my forehead and whisper, "I'm so stupid!"

"No." Mom's voice softens, and she holds my hands in hers. "You are not stupid. You've juggled a lot this summer, and you've done it brilliantly. And I'm not just saying that because you're my daughter."

"What should I do?"

She thinks a minute. "Well...it can be short. Everyone wants to eat. The fewer words the better."

"But what should those few words be?"

"Ask God to bless the marriage. That's what I'd do."

"That's what a priest would do." I see Joshua waving at

me to come to the head table. Eden and Justin are already seated. "Can you think of a short poem or something?"

She shakes her head. "The only thing that comes to mind is the theme song from that kid's show with the purple dinosaur. The 'I love you, you love me' thing." She hugs me again. "Speak from the heart, and it'll be perfect. I promise."

"I think I'm going to throw up."

"Honey, trust me. You can't go wrong with 'God bless this marriage.'"

I take my seat next to Eden. Like royalty, the bridal party is served first. I'm starving, but I can't eat. My mind races for words, but now the stupid Barney song is stuck in my head.

Finally Joshua stands and clinks his glass with a fork to get everyone's attention. "On behalf of my entire family, I thank you all for being with us on this important day." He looks at Justin. "I can honestly say I've never seen my brother so happy. Eden is the kindest person I've ever met, and we're thrilled to have her in our family. Join me in toasting my brother and his wife."

Glasses clink, and Joshua gives me a nod.

It's my turn.

Mom was right. A few words worked just fine. All I

have to do is use Joshua's words, but change them around. As soon as I stand up, my mind goes blank. I can't even remember the best man's name. Jerry? Jasper? I can't remember Mom's words. Something about God and a purple dinosaur. I'm sweating buckets and teetering on my heels. Four words cycle through my head: *Don't. Lock. The. Knees.*

Everyone stares, waiting for me to say something. Mom and Dad are at the table closest to the front, so I look at them for strength, and they give me confident smiles. Luke isn't paying attention. He's too busy balancing the spoon on his nose. And next to Luke is Nick.

Nick! What's he doing here? He doesn't even look mad. He looks happy. He leans forward and quietly mouths, "Don't dilly dally."

That boy is a genius. He pulled me right out of panic mode with a simple joke. I take the deepest possible breath and find my voice. "Eden is the best cousin in the world. Now I have to share her with Justin, and I'm okay with that, because she's happy." I bite my lip and think. "And I'm getting another cousin out of the deal, because now Justin's part of our family. And..." I should've stopped there. Why'd I go and add an "and"? "... and our family is a little...interesting..." I hold up my arms, look down at the dress, and everybody laughs. I got a laugh! "…and I'm glad we're interesting and…" Why'd I go and add *another* "and"? I'm lost in the middle of this sentence, so I look at Mom and quickly say, "…and may God bless this marriage."

I sit down as fast as possible, and everyone claps and clinks glasses.

Eden leans toward me and whispers, "Rock star."

After dinner, I scan the crowd for Nick and find him near the dance floor, watching the band members tune their instruments. I tap his shoulder, and he turns around and laughs when he sees me. "I didn't know junior bridesmaids wore white."

"Didn't you learn about Catholic wedding customs during your religion class?"

"Good one." He shifts awkwardly on his feet. "This wedding is awesome. You could go viral."

"That's what I was thinking."

"I'm not a wedding crasher. Your grandma came over last night and invited me."

"Oh. I'm glad." Wedding talk is tough. I'd give anything to have a basketball or skateboard in my hand. I'm stumped, so I say, "Did you like the chicken?"

"The chicken? Yeah, it was good."

"Good. I'm glad."

"Me, too."

I'm doing it again—I'm not saying what I'm thinking. Because what I'm thinking is I'm sorry, and I want to be friends. I take a deep breath. Nothing can be worse than giving a toast, so I just blurt out the words. "I'm sorry about the Communion thing."

"So am I."

Nick looks really relieved I started this conversation, and I'm not done. "Nick, will you think I'm stupid if I still believe in miracles?"

"Like Jesus coming back from the dead and all that?"

"Like that."

"Well, there must be miracles in this world because you're wearing the bride's dress, and your grandma hasn't fired lightning bolts from her eyes." I laugh, and he says, "If you believe in miracles, I'm cool with that. Just don't give up on science."

"Of course not! Maybe I'll be a scientist someday. I like science."

"You could be a scientist. You're like the smartest person I know." He tucks his hands into his pockets and raises his eyebrows. "But I'm the best dancer."

The singer strums his guitar and calls Eden and Uncle Will to the dance floor. Nick and I perch near the speaker. The dance begins with the song "In My Life" by the Beatles. Eden and Uncle Will grip each other's shoulders and rock back and forth. The motion is so stiff they look like they might tip over. Then the singer says they're going to play "You Are Wonderful Tonight," and that this dance is just for the bride and groom. Eden and Justin sort of melt together, cheek to cheek, and sway. I'm sure about one thing: When they're together, they are comfortable in their awkwardness.

About halfway through the song, the singer says the rest of the bridal party should join the bride and groom. I'm embarrassed, but I take Joshua's hand and put as much distance between us as possible while keeping my arm on his shoulder. After another verse, the singer invites everyone to the dance floor. Joshua pats me on the shoulder, says, "Nice job, Mary," and lets go.

I'm about to make my escape from the dance floor, but Nick is still standing by the speaker. He sees that I'm watching him. One of us has to take the first step. One of us has to say something about dancing together.

I guess it's up to me.

"So," I say, "you said you liked to dance."

"Actually, I said I was the best dancer, which is a complete and total lie. It just sort of flew out of my mouth, you know? I was thinking I'd hide in the bathroom until it's over."

"We could just sit at a table and watch."

He seems relieved for a second, but he shakes his head. "That'd be lame, don't you think?"

"So you do want to dance? Or you don't?"

"I'll dance unless you don't want to."

I yank his arm and pull him to the dance floor, and we're dancing. We're swaying side to side like the other dancers. It's not too weird. Actually, it's not weird at all.

And the music stops. Our hands have been pressed together for ten whole seconds.

He laughs. "Told you. I'm amazing."

The singer tells everyone young and old to get to the dance floor for the "Hokey Pokey," which is a silly and ridiculous song, but at least I know how to do it. You're *supposed* to look ridiculous doing the "Hokey Pokey." It's almost the point. Also, we don't have to hold hands, which is the good part and the bad part.

As the music starts, Luke darts across the room to get in the center of the action. Eden walks to Grandma and holds out her hand. Grandma takes it. They stand side by side, next to Luke, and wait for the singer's instructions.

Eden does not change her mind and flee the dance floor. With her arm wrapped around Grandma, Eden puts her right foot in and then out and then in and, no kidding, Eden actually shakes it all about. Justin leans against the speaker and claps. My parents and Aunt Maggie and Uncle Will leave their drinks on the table and join the circle.

We hokey pokey—all of us.

ABOUT BRENT HELZINSKI AND ME

DOES ANYONE PRAY FOR BRENT HELZINSKI?

I do.